The Last Christmas of Ebenezer Scrooge

The Last Christmas of Ebenezer Scrooge

Marvin Kaye

WILDSIDE PRESS

**THE LAST CHRISTMAS
OF EBENEZER SCROOGE**

An original publiation of
Wildside Press
www.wildsidepress.com

10 9 8 7 6 5 4 3 2

To
My Wonderful Daughter
TERRY ELLEN KAYE
whose performance in
a production of
A CHRISTMAS CAROL
first gave me this idea

Prelude

THE OLD MAN IN THE WINDOW

To Paulie, the chance meeting with the old man in the window was a turning-point in his life. Yet a distant onlooker might have dismissed the incident as the most trivial of encounters.

The fact that it was Christmas meant nothing to the nine-year-old. It was just another bitter December day to endure and get through. That morning, winter sun sparkled on diamond-bright London rooftops. A frore wind sent chalky grains down roads so sharply etched in morning light that their edges might have been cut with the gleaming blade of a French barber's polished shaving tool.

Hordes of gentlemen in velvet greatcoats, fur-collared, wore tall dome hats and proffered gloved hands to virtuous maidens, escorting them across icy sidewalks and into whichever waiting churches they deemed individually most proper. Switching aside wildernesses of crinolines, the women settled onto unpillowed, polished pews, buffered by the copious billows of their finery. The men, doffing tall hats, sat rigidly erect, clutching serried ranks of gold-handled walking sticks.

Outside, the skinless air shook with an artillery of steeple-bells, as an army of sextons tolled Christmas chimes that comforted the hearts of the comfortable worshippers.

But the clamour fell harshly on the ears of the residents of one East End road within the auditory compass of St. Alban's Cathedral. Little wider than an alley, it was a narrow, dirty street flooded with slush that slopped over kerbs and stained the tattered shoes of its itinerant inhabitants; the cracked and crooked paving angled with the twistings of the garbage-cobbled street. Barrowe Lane consisted of dingy shops and grimy dwelling-hovels; squat, smoky piles that told of rooms "to let" on rusted shingles hung outside. Grey was the dominant shade, winter and summer; the hue of sunless afternoons, of chimney-pots unscoured and walkways crackling with grit underfoot. The flats vied for space with the cramped shops of clothing-menders, cabinet-makers, boot and shoe cobblers, none of whom honoured this (or any other) Christmas Day.

The residents of Barrowe Lane were like the street, and included many bleak specimens of humanity. The coldest and grimmest of all was the widow Gamwell, a stout woman of sixty years who wore her grey hair in a loose knot and her pinched lips in a tight frown.

But that morning, as the massive landlady opened the front door of the building she rented and ventured forth onto the slippery sidewalk, her pasty face sported an uncommon smile. Sniffing in derision at the distant peal of bells, she smoothed the gaudy bodice of her chintz dress. Her squat nose caught the heady savour of fresh-baked loaves from Patchin's bake-house; the odour almost succeeded in covering the stench of Barrowe Lane.

Clutching a small wad of bills and coins in her stubby fingers, she stepped off in the direction of the bake-house, and as she did she stuck the cash in her fist into the large pocket of her dress.

At the same moment, not far away, another hand, withered and bony, rummaged in a purse and withdrew a small handful.

"Count it over, Pasey-Paulie, see how much is left," she told her son.

The child took the money and spread it out on the floor beneath a high, barred window-grate, the only source of light in the heatless basement. Once a year in late spring, the landlady hired a ladder and had the grating cleaned, but even then it shed little brightness on the broken plaster walls. Before Paulie's father died, they had candles to combat the gloom, but he was gone and Paulie's mother was too sick to work. In the dusty sunlight that filtered into the chilly cellar, Paulie squinted as his shivering fingers counted out the coins, one by one.

"Not only wouldn't she wait, she raised the rent another shilling," his mother explained, though Paulie needed no explanation. She lay back against a pile of rags in the corner, coughing. Paulie guessed the source of the meager cache: each week, when she had still been able to work, his mother must have cheated her own slender frame of sustenance so she could feed her son. *Foolish*, he thought. *Not practical.*

Paulie announced the meager sum. His mother wrote a list, kissed him on the cheek, told him to take the order to the grocer's, then lay down, only to struggle up on one elbow when the coughing seized and shook her.

Paulie knew he must do something. He donned the jacket of his best suit, an action the darkness hid from her weak eyes.

"Paulie!" Outside, someone called his name. Looking up, he saw the thin old tailor, Simon Besserman, who several times a day scuttled bent-kneed from shop to room, because the former lacked the sanitary necessities contained in the latter. He stooped to tousle Paulie's hair.

"Why such a face, boy?"

"Mrs. Gamwell raised our rent again."

"Ach, Paulie, when a Jew collects rent, he becomes a goy! But how's your Momma?"

"She can't stop coughing."

"In a winter like this — !" The tailor produced an iron key from his vest, locked his shop-door and stepped off into the street. "Listen, Paulie . . . a little hot tea is what your Momma needs. Wait, wait, I'll be right back!" He scurried across the lane to his shop, went into the room where he lived and came out presently with a scrap of paper folded around a few spoons of tea. He pressed the packet into the child's hands. "Hot tea will break up the cough. You'll see!"

Paulie thanked him and walked off, hands in pockets, partly for warmth, partly to keep the weight of his thin arm and the tea packet pressed securely against the money in his jacket. He was wearing a holiday suit, but the knees and elbows were shiny, the cuffs frayed. He hoped the worn places would not be too obvious.

Abel Troster, the grocer, lived with his younger brother David, their shapeless wives and a combined muster of fourteen children in a double-duty business and residence that might have served as the temporary lodging for a childless couple. The grocer was a portly man of fifty; his brother David, though two years younger, seemed the older because of his bald head and wizened body.

Although the grocery was prudently closed on Christmas morning, the large grocer opened the door for Paulie. Tracing a ragged finger-nail down the list the boy handed him, he checked off items, occasionally calling some question to his brother in the back.

"So, Paulie?" the large man asked, glancing down at the boy. "How's your mother?"

"Not so good."

David clucked dolefully from the rear of the store, but Abel waved an imperious finger and restored silence.

"Well, Paulie," the senior grocer rumbled, "your mother should eat some of my Sadie's chicken soup, she'll feel much better. David will bring over your order, and he'll also bring you a pot of soup, hot off the stove."

David shouted, "Don't forget to bring back the pot, Paulie!"

"Duvid, don't be a shlemiel!" Abel Troster shouted back. "He's going to carry a pot twice his size?" He patted Paulie's cheek. "Tomorrow, Duvid will get the pot. Give Mama a big hug."

Paulie thanked him and left, biting his lip. He appreciated his neighbour's kindness, but his mother was too sick to be helped by a cup of tea or even a bowl of what his father used to call the best chicken soup in the world.

Mama needs medicine!

"It's Christmas, brat, *go away!*"

"But my mother is sick!"

Cracking the front door to let him in, the tall chemist told Paulie to describe her symptoms. He spoke in a dry, rasping voice; a mirthless smile and hawk nose hung beneath cold grey eyes that fixed the child like a butterfly stuck on a specimen-pin.

As Paulie described his mother's illness, he couldn't help but gaze in wonder at the vaulting piles of books and brazen utensils, at the high shelves crammed with turquoise and amber bottles of mysterious powders and potions, anywhere but into the hard, cold eyes of the apothecary.

As he spoke, the chemist examined with disfavour the boy's patched, worn clothing. When Paulie was finished, he did not reply, but turned and puttered in the back of the store, in a moment returning with a small phial of colourless liquid, which he placed on the counter-top.

"This will cure your mother. She must mix it in water and take it twice a day, in the morning and at vespers."

"V-vespers?" The word was new to Paulie.

Ignoring the question, the druggist told Paulie the price of the elixir. The lad's face fell; he was precisely one half-crown short. But he placed what money he had on the counter and waited while the old man prodded the coins with crooked, bony fingers. Suddenly he glared at the boy with narrowed eyes.

"You're shy half-a-crown!" he growled, grabbing Paulie roughly by the shoulder. "Did you think I wouldn't see, scamp?"

"Please," he pleaded, trying to free himself from the crab-pinch grip, "just sell me as much as I can buy with —!"

A vicious shake. "I don't like lads who try to cheat me."

"But the medicine —"

"Costs half-a-crown more!" He pushed Paulie back so hard he stumbled. "I'll be here two more hours, then I'm going to church. Bring me the balance by noon, and your mother shall have her medi-

cine. If you don't return in time, I'll keep this, I will."
He swept the coins into the pocket of his apron.

It was useless to protest. Paulie assured the chemist he would bring him the rest of the money. The old man's rejoinder pierced his ears like barbs.

"Of course you will. Jews breed cash like lice."

Paulie's decision to appropriate the last bit of money to buy medicine was not motivated by sentiment, he told himself. The fact that he loved his mother meant little; what *was* important was that she was too sick to work. No money was coming into the household. Thus it was simple common sense to obtain medicine that would restore her health; then she could once again seek employment, and the two of them would be able to eat. Had his father been alive, Paulie was certain he would have approved of the responsibility his son was assuming.

But how can I get half-a-crown by noon?

Communing with himself, the child walked down a broad snowy avenue, his face turned to the biting wind. Morning services were half-over; all the bells were stilled. As he slogged along, he practically had the sidewalk to himself. The only other travellers were delivery boys. Frost reddened Paulie's cheeks and chapped his lips. His feet crunched crisply on the pavement's frozen crust. It was ten-fifteen. Half-a-crown — a niggling amount, but it never occurred to Paulie to ask someone for it. Raised in his father's strict ethic, he knew that to want money was to earn it: no charity, but honest wages.

But in the scant time he had, what could a nine-year-old do? The shops were closed, only the bakeries were open. Maybe one of them needed an extra delivery boy? Or perhaps some master-chef, busy with preparations for a festive dinner, might find himself suddenly caught short of some essential herb at the penultimate turn of the spit. *But how do I find somebody like that?*

Paulie looked about for an open shop: at first he thought he was in luck, for there was a bakery in the next block doing brisk holiday business. But as he approached, he saw that the people streaming in and out of doors consisted solely of livery-clad servants transporting cakes and breads to various destinations.

He wandered up and down empty Christmas streets, but all was silent snow and shut-up windows. Time sped on; ten-thirty, ten-fifty. Fortune would not favour the child's quest.

Just as the clocks struck eleven, Paulie spied a large, bustling shop some distance away. He ran towards it. It was on a dreary street of banks and fiduciary offices. Across the way, a small church was just letting out a stream of happy morning worshippers. Here and there he saw town-houses set back from the street, guarded by iron gates; Gothic eyries that seemed fit haunts for companies of spectres.

The poulterer's, which occupied the largest corner space of a particularly dreary block, considerably brightened the neighbourhood. Its windows were festooned with colourful banners, geese and sausages, hams and fowl so immense they dwarfed the lad as he gazed up in open-mouthed wonder.

The doors were open; the air was filled with a cacophony of cackling voices. Hordes of caterers, cooks and chefs jammed the store's interior, jostling one another as they prodded fowl and haggled with the clerks over prices and pounds.

"That's seven and six. Where shall we deliver?"

"Lookit! Mind where you're steppin'!"

"I've *got* to 'ave a twelve-pounder, I tells yer!"

Paulie pushed his way into the crowd, which swallowed him up without a trace. Elbows jammed into his face; someone's knee struck him in the middle of his back. A fat chef tramped on Paulie's toes. Shoved and bruised by the press of giant bodies, the little boy raised his voice in a thin wail that almost went unheard in the jabbering gabble of birds and people.

But at the front of the market, the master butcher, a lean, stringy gentleman with fierce moustaches and ebony spit-curls plastered to his forehead, heard the whining plaint. Bawling an order to an underling in a military bray, he rounded the counter and saw a small pair of eyes peering out between the flanks of two rotund customers.

"'ere, boy!" he shouted. "What do you want?"

"I want to speak to the head butcher!" Paulie

cried over the din.

"That's me," the moustached man replied in a tone that defied anyone to disagree. "What do you want?"

"Do you need a delivery boy?"

"What in 'ell do you think this is, a bloody employment office?" the butcher howled, thrusting his bristly face inches away from the frightened boy. "Get out!"

"But I need money *now!*"

"My God," the master butcher said in a bray that everyone could hear, "they start the ruddy beggars young!"

His comment met with a vociferous chorus of assent. Paulie, cheeks burning with shame, turned and tried to run; unfortunately, retreat was as difficult and bruising as his entry had been. At last he broke free and stumbled into the street.

The child told himself he was not going to cry, yet found it hard to keep from trembling. Though he lived in a poor neighbourhood, Paulie was unused to abuse. Before his father fled Poland, he had been a man of means, and in the little world that was Barrowe Lane, this still had some meaning, so Paulie, consequently, had been spared the harsher buffets of "polite society."

The quarter-hour chimed. Paulie mastered his emotions. He had no business thinking of his own feelings when his mother's health was at stake. By this time, he was afraid she might be worried at his prolonged absence, but he had no choice but to continue with his quest. Less than an hour remained before the chemist closed his doors; how *could* he earn that crucial half-crown?

The scene in the poultry shop flashed before his eyes. Suddenly, a new thought struck him; he thrust it away, but it returned with renewed force.

The butcher had called him a *beggar* . . .

He pictured the shock on his father's face if he suspected what his son was thinking. Yet Paulie was pragmatic; his father was dead, would never know. As for his mother, he simply wouldn't tell her — and yet, why did he hesitate? Was it pride? How could he let that stop him, when his mother was sick in bed, perhaps —

Paulie vigorously shook his head, trying to clear it of the unwelcome thought. He studied the wealthy congregants milling about the church across the street, and tried to calculate how long it might take him to wheedle half-a-crown from their holiday purses. It was not a time for internal harangue; Talmudic hair-splittings of family duty *vs.* family duty. Paulie made up his mind in an instant, and his only regret was that he wasn't wearing a cap to catch the largesse he hoped these Christians might dispense.

By the time the half-hour chimed, the cluster of worshippers had disappeared. Paulie stepped across the street, stuffing booty in his jacket pockets. He wondered whether the luxuriously-cloaked gentlemen would have been quite so generous if they'd met him on a hurried homeward journey from their places of employment, rather than Christmas morning in front of church with smiling maidens by their sides. But for whatever reasons, they had treated the waif handsomely, and the flow of cash tinkled gaily into the gloveless palms of the supplicating youth.

Entering a narrow side-street, Paulie thanked heaven for the manna bestowed on him. The money he'd begged would be more than enough for medicine; ample funds would be left to feed him and his mother for several days to come, and by that time, she would surely —

The thought was choked out with his breath. A dark figure shot out of the black doorway of an empty house; before Paulie could utter a sound, he was shoved against a wall.

Clawing desperately at the hands gripping his throat, Paulie beat his fists against the assailant, but with no effect. The other, relinquishing his strangle-hold, clapped a rough hand over Paulie's mouth and warned him not to cry out. Then he cautiously released him.

His attacker was a chunky boy of fifteen. He wore ragged trousers, a woolen scarf and a thick sailor's jacket. Beneath an unruly mat of pale yellow hair, a pair of sharp black eyes glinted out like twin points of a pitchfork. He towered over Paulie.

"'Oo yer workin' for?"

Paulie glanced round fearfully. Although he was only a block from the church-steps, he might have been in some foreign counry. The street was deserted, its houses boarded up. Nothing moved except paper-scraps fluttering in the wind.

The older boy's mouth twisted into a belligerent sneer. "I said, 'oo yer workin' for?"

"No-one," Paulie replied, terrified.

It was just the answer his tormentor wanted to hear. Without another word, he shoved his big hands into Paulie's pockets and began to take the coins and bills inside. The tea packet burst open.

"Let go! *It's for my mother's medicine!*"

The hooligan shoved him and Paulie's head smacked something hard; his knees buckled. The other pushed him sideways to the ground. After that, it was the work of a few seconds to rob the child of his beggar's wages.

When he was done, the rough leaned down so his face loomed inches away from Paulie's. "Where yer from?"

"B-Barrowe Lane," he stammered.

"Next time y' beg, do it there, Jew-boy. Crooknoses better stay out of *our* neighbourhood!" He emphasized this lesson in ethnic protocol by kicking his victim in the ribs before wandering off.

Paulie lay in the snow a long time, refusing to shed tears. Except for a dull ache in his chest, the physical pain had subsided. Only one injury still ached: in his mind he heard, over and over, the vile expectoration of a word he'd been taught to regard with pride and respect.

What made these people treat him with such contempt? Did the ghetto cling to his old, frayed clothes, offending Gentile noses with its telltale reek? Or was it the creed his father raised him in? Was he stamped with an invisible Mark of Cain, the odious child of an intolerable people?

Brushing himself off, Paulie rose and began to walk home. The tumble in the snow had thoroughly chilled him, and he was colder still within. It was too late, he knew, to find work and he dare not beg again, which meant that the chemist would keep the rest of the money, and Paulie's mother would never get her vital medicine. And without it . . .

Without it . . .

NO!

Something broke inside Paulie; a scream that stopped up the tears he could not, would not shed. In that instant, born of desperation, an awful idea stabbed him like a jagged splinter.

His father's face flashed into his mind, but he had already cried over him to no purpose, for tears and prayers could not bring back the dead. With less difficulty than the boy might have imagined, Paulie banished the image, all thought of paternal precept now buried in the urgent need to examine this dreadfully necessary new plan.

Mama needs medicine. The chemist has the kind she needs. I know which bottle he keeps it in. In less than half-an-hour, the shop will close, he told me so, and its windows, he reasoned, *are only made of glass . . .*

As the forbidden thought raced through his mind, Paulie left the deserted street and entered a quiet square with a massive, ugly town-house on one corner. The baleful edifice, fronted by a barren patch that once was a plot of long-dead grass, was shut off from the thoroughfare by a wrought-iron gate. High in the side of the house overlooking the street a narrow, peaked casement lowered; in itself it possessed nothing of the marvellous.

And then it happened.

An old man in a night-cap and dressing-gown pushed the window up with such force that the bang resounded throughout the square.

Startled by the noise, Paulie craned his neck and saw a gentleman most remarkable to behold: he had a pointed nose, thin lips and sharp chin; a face so angular it resembled a cluster of icicles. Yet there was a merry gleam in his eye, and peal upon peal of the heartiest laughter issued from his wrinkled lips. Suddenly noticing the child, the old man waved his hand and called out to him, but he was too high above Paulie's head to be heard, so he shouted louder.

"What's to-day, my fine fellow?"

The compliment pleased Paulie, but the bleak recollection that it was Christmas hardened his heart. He suddenly hated the holiday and its wealthy celebrants who by now were probably sitting down to sumptuous repasts while his mother lay starving, wasted by disease. Still, he shouted up the requested information, "Christmas Day!" allowing the irony of the notion to crowd from his consciousness an increasingly insistent thought.

Bellowing in order to be heard, the odd old man in the window asked whether Paulie knew "the poulterer's in the next street but one, at the corner?"

"I should hope I did!" he replied ruefully.

The zany muttered something Paulie could not hear, then raised his voice once more. "Do you know whether they've sold the prize turkey that was hanging up there? — Not the little prize turkey: the big one?"

"What! The one as big as me?"

The old man nodded.

"It's hanging there now," the boy replied.

"Is it? Go and buy it."

That was utter nonsense and Paulie said as much.

"No, no," the old man cried. "I am in earnest. Go and buy it, and tell 'em to bring it here, that I may give them the directions where to take it. Come back with the man, and I'll give you a shilling —"

Paulie, not believing his ears, held his breath.

"Come back with him in less than five minutes,"

the old man shouted gleefully with much head-wag-gling and grinning, "and I'll give you *half-a-crown!*"

At the magic words, the boy sped off. He must have had a steady hand at a trigger who could have got a shot off half as fast. Taking giant leaps, Paulie ran in the street, where his feet had better pur-chase. Nonetheless, he took several spills, none of which he paid any attention to; scrambling erect again, he sped along, sliding, trotting, hopping, skipping, scampering sometimes on all fours, until at last he raced pell-mell through the door of the poultry-shop. The place was still as crowded, but this time, the lad employed elbows and feet, knees and fists, even, regrettably, his teeth. At the cost of a few hearty buffets and curses, Paulie forced his way to the front of the store, where he tugged insistently at the master butcher's apron.

"What in 'ell do *you* want?"

Paulie told him.

"What?!" the butcher snapped, eyes goggling in disbelief. Sweeping his hand in the direction of the main window, he asked, "Am I to understand you want to buy *that* turkey?"

"Yes, sir!"

"Do you 'ear this?" the man blustered in a voice so loud that all the clerks and shoppers stopped to listen. "Scarce an hour ago, this wee rascal comes in beggin' me for a job. And now he's got the colossal cheek to return and say that 'e wants to buy me prize turkey!"

"Why, the shrimp couldn't even carry it!" a fat caterer observed.

"You don't understand!" Paulie protested. "It's not for me! The old man in the big house two blocks away wants to buy it!"

"What old man is that?" the butcher asked suspiciously. "Which 'ouse d'ye mean?"

Paulie began to describe the house and the man. In haste to return before the five minutes elapsed, he stumbled over his words, but managed to blurt it all out breathlessly.

As he spoke, the butcher exchanged knowing glances with his customers. Somebody started to giggle. A clerk took it up. The sound grew into a guffaw. By the time Paulie finished, the room rocked with wild, derisive laughter.

The master butcher's strident bray rose above the din. "I've 'eard it all now! A Christmas turkey for Old Scratch hisself! Of all people — 'IM!!!"

But Paulie hardly noticed the laughter because he was listening to something else. In the distance, the church-bells were striking the hour of noon.

When the laughter died down, a new sound could be heard in the poultry shop. A serving-man tittered, but half-a-dozen people shushed him. The butcher, no longer smiling, squatted on his haunches next to Paulie and spoke to him in a voice that did not bray at all.

"Now then, young man, don't take on like that. I meant no harm." The unexpected kindness made

Paulie rest his head upon the man's broad breast. Circling the small, sobbing shoulders, the master butcher patted the child's back. "There now, lad, there now, tell me what's troubling you."

"My mother," Paulie sobbed. "She — she's going to *die* . . ."

When the old man saw Paulie and the delivery boy coming, he gave out a merry whoop. He was standing next to his front door still clad in night-dress and cap. One hand rested affectionately on the massive knocker affixed to the door.

"Here's the turkey," he laughed. "Hallo! Merry Christmas! Why, it's impossible to carry that to Camden Town. You must have a cab." The chuckle with which he said this, and the chuckle with which he paid for the turkey, were only exceeded by the chuckle with which he paid for the cab.

Once the great fowl was despatched, Paulie approached with hand outstretched to claim his reward. The old man, already groping in the pocket of his gown for half-a-crown, suddenly shivered as he saw the child draw near. The smile on his lips disappeared; he shrank back involuntarily.

Paulie's spirits sank. *He won't pay me!*

But then the smile returned to the old man's lips. To Paulie's inestimable surprise, he bowed to him. "My deepest apologies, young man. My eyes are weak, and for a moment you reminded me of a dreadful child I saw in a nightmare — but of course,

I was only being foolish. Come closer, let me look at you."

Paulie complied. The old man ran his crooked fingers down the sleeve of the child's jacket. "When I hailed you from the window, I took this suit for holiday finery. But now I see it's tattered and patched." He bent down so he could look straight into Paulie's eyes. "Tell me, child, where is your coat? It's much too cold to be out the way you're dressed."

Encouraged by the old man's sympathetic tone, in a great rush of words Paulie embarked upon the story of his poverty. He told of his father's death and his mother's illness, of the freezing cellar where she lay sick, of his attempt to buy her medicine, and all of the troubles and abuse he'd experienced that morning.

When he was done, the old man did a most peculiar thing: he danced. Not a formal ballroom set of figures, but a wild caper all around the yard. Cracking his knees almost double, he leaped gaily about, kicking up flurries of snow-flakes with his slippered feet. And while he cavorted, he chuckled, giggled and whooped like a drunkard in a wine-vault.

Paulie was deeply hurt by this callous reception of his tale, which the old man seemed to find sublimely funny. But suddenly, observing the somber look upon the child's face, the white-haired caperer ceased his antics and, kneeling down beside the child, lightly rested withered hands on Paulie's small shoulders.

"Don't despise me, lad," he implored. "I felt as if a heavy burden were lifted from my spirit, and I simply had to dance! But hearken to me! How is this for an agenda? I'll shave and dress, and we'll fetch a cab to call upon your mother. We'll find a suitable inn where the two of you may grow warm and comfortable till I can set my clerk to procure for you some pleasant, more permanent abode. Good victuals we'll purchase, and as soon as the stores are open, a thick coat to guard you from this bitter chill. But the very, very first thing we'll do is summon the best physicians we can find, even if we have to pull them away from their Christmas dinners! Now how does all that sound to start with, eh?"

"But why," asked Paulie, tears in his eyes, "why do you want to do all this for me? Don't you know?"

"Don't I know what?"

"We live in Barrowe Lane." Lowering his voice to a murmur, he added, "I . . . I'm a Jew."

"Yes, I know," the other replied gently. "So was my partner, God rest his soul." Stroking once more the massive knocker on his front door, the old man shook his head and sighed.

"God rest his soul," repeated Scrooge.

Later that day, riding to Barrowe Lane in a cab, an exciting adventure for a little boy, Paulie pointed out the chemist's shop as they rode past.

"*That* vile apothecary!" his companion snorted.

"Damme, I know him well: he would have sold you a beakerful of water!" Suddenly, a surprised expression appeared upon the old man's face, and he began to shake with merriment.

"What's so funny?" Paulie asked.

"The chemist!" the old man laughed. "I believe . . . *I* hold his mortgage!"

Stave One

THE BEGINNING OF IT

benezer Scrooge notwithstanding, it is the rare individual who alters his nature overnight, and society, in the lump, never does. The rebellion that broke the peace at Boston Harbour was aged in Gallic casques to be decanted at Spithead and the Nore in coastal mutinies that elevated the Rights of Man above England's security. Seven decades later, Parliament, hard-pressed to redefine what it means to be a British citizen, argued the question of its own qualifying oath, and only after years of bitter protest that such an act would compromise the ethical underpinnings of a Christian nation was Baron Lionel de Rothschild, the first Jew to be elected to the House of Commons, permitted to be sworn in upon the Old Testament, rather than the New.

Another statesman once observed that while social institutions may give the illusion of permanency, nothing in life is certain except death and taxes, and yet the passage through time of men and nations suggests a third constant: that of immutable change. Only because Time, that indefatigable labourer, works slowly, does it seem that wealth, government and its temporal wisdom shall forever endure. Fleeting, immutable change; and though we seek something sure and beautiful and lasting, yet the best of hearts must break upon the shoals of that continent called Tomorrow.

And so it came to pass that the great reformation of Ebenezer Scrooge, like every event memorable or mundane, bygone or yet to be, was duly noted in the City, duly laughed at, then duly forgotten. Hours ran into days, days lumped into weeks, weeks added up to months, months amassed into years, and those who scoffed at Scrooge's reclamation were dim of memory and few in number.

One Michaelmas eve, that feast which marks the close of the year's third quarter, Ebenezer Scrooge stood outside his warehouse in the company of his nephew Fred, Bob Cratchit, Mrs. Cratchit and the many members of the Cratchit clan. The weather was bleak and biting. Every one beat their hands upon their breasts and stamped their feet on the paving stones as they looked up expectantly at the building's veiled upper face.

Scrooge nodded to his nephew Fred, who hauled at a stout rope. The canvas that concealed the warehouse wall pulled away, and after a moment of hushed delight, the thin air crackled with the choppy applause of chapped hands.

Timothy Cratchit, a handsome lad in his teens, bright of eye, tall and straight-standing (though he leaned upon a thick ash walking-stick), gently tugged his parent's arm.

"Father," said he, "you may open your eyes."

Bob Cratchit, whose apple-cheek plumpness made him look more like Timothy's elder brother, did as his son suggested. With a broad grin, he lifted his chin and beheld for the first time the bright, new-painted sign set high on the building's façade:

Of late, Scrooge had been uncommonly melancholy, but this day he was determined to put on a brave front. "A prosperous life to you, partner Bob!" he said, clapping him on the back. "And now, let us all celebrate this grand, auspicious occasion with a bowl of smoking bishop and a hearty dinner! The owner of the last foot to arrive at the inn must foot the bill!"

With much laughter and hugging, the celebrants adjourned as Scrooge proposed.

Eleven years had come and gone since the morning of Scrooge's Grand Epiphany. In that time, he had never veered from his new philanthropic course; this must be distinctly understood, or nothing wonderful can come of this tale. Scrooge kept the spirit of Christmas in his heart. All his Yuletides he passed with his family, feasting and playing games with children and grown-ups alike, and each Christmas Eve his nephew's wife would bestow upon Scrooge a dainty press of her hand and a kiss upon his cheek, and the unvarying proclamation that there was roast goose and pudding, "and Topper said he'd come, so we'll raise our glasses, and our voices, too, in song!" and Scrooge was always the last to leave the party, for then he had the opportunity of distributing his gifts beneath the great tree dominating the parlour.

If in his latter-day devotion to the principles of charity, Ebenezer Scrooge somewhat neglected his own business (and he did), his new partner Bob Cratchit courted it assiduously. Pundits declared that "the old sinner must be making up for lost time," yet even they admitted Scrooge appeared to have struck some kind of divine balance, for the more money he devoted to the needy, the more it poured into his firm's coffers.

And yet lately the old man's spirit had grown restless; his slumbers were troubled and his moods were melancholy.

"Is it any wonder, uncle? Look where you live!" His nephew Fred repeatedly urged him to quit his gloomy digs and move in with his family.

"My home," Scrooge argued, "belonged to my poor friend Jacob Marley, who saved me from his own bitter fate on these very premises."

"You've told me so on many occasions." To Fred's credit, he did not stress the word *many,* except perhaps in his own mind. But his efforts on the question of improved living quarters were unflagging, and so were the sweet entreaties of his little daughter Fan, who reminded Scrooge of another time and place and person. At length the old man consented, with a major stipulation: that he would procure and furnish a larger home for Fred and his family, Scrooge included, to live in. Fred did not wish to accept such a generous gift, but, perceiving it as the only way

Scrooge would quit his somber apartments, he and his wife reluctantly agreed.

Forthwith, Bob Cratchit was assigned the task of finding a suitable property, which he soon secured in a fashionable new quarter of London that was recommended to him by Mr. Veneering, the middle partner of Chicksey, Veneering & Stobbles, a Mincing Lane establishment that Scrooge, Marley, & Cratchit sometimes did business with, and in this fashion it came to pass that Ebenezer Scrooge and his kinfolk, old and young, came to reside under the same roof.

Now Scrooge's new bedroom was cozy and comfortable, yet he enjoyed little rest therein. Fred, perceiving his uncle's disquietude, attributed it to the move itself, for change, even that which we encompass in our hopes, exacts a toll upon our faculties. Scrooge, however, since bidding farewell to his old digs, was as robust as one might reasonably expect in one of his advanced years. If he sensed his own gradual decline, and he did, his faith shielded him from fearing his dwindling time on earth.

Yet though his body was hale and his mind composed, Scrooge's dreams were disturbed by strange landscapes, portents and events he could not recall when he woke. In bed, he twisted, tossed and turned, and greeted the dawn with a groan.

His nephew had observed his kinsman's unease for some days. Fred's wife prompted him to inquire into the cause, but Fred was loath to do so, reasoning that although Ebenezer Scrooge had long ago given up his secret, solitary ways, he still was a man of business who'd spent most of his life keeping his own counsel.

But the morning after the new company sign was unveiled, Scrooge himself resolved to speak to Fred. At the end of breakfast, having considered his words carefully, he caught his eye and beckoned him into the parlour. Shutting the door, Scrooge, with lowered voice, said, "Fred, lately my spirit has been troubled. I've been having bad dreams."

"Nightmares?"

"I can't remember them." Scrooge stroked his wiry chin. "I think they are very sad."

"I'll summon Doctor Hopkins."

Scrooge protested that his discomfort was of the mind, but Fred affectionately patted his shoulder. "Uncle, you've often remarked on the linkage of spirit and flesh. That story you've told us about your partner's ghost . . . 'There's more of gravy than of grave . . . a bit of undigested potato.'"

Scrooge chuckled. "Hoist by mine own petard."

Now there is a breed of physicians whose professional heartiness disposes them to address patients as if they were all hard of hearing, and Dr. Jack Hopkins was of that number. There was no action that a fly-weight practitioner might accomplish softly that Dr. Hopkins would not render noisily: he set his instruments down with a smack, rattled his black bag when he walked, and strode along with such foot-stamping energy as might put a marching army to shame.

A clattering cab brought Dr. Hopkins to the door, which he whacked with a resounding triple-knock that shook the portal. He arrived clad in a blue striped shirt with a white false collar, and a black velvet waist-coat with thunder-and-lightning buttons.

Fred escorted the physician to his uncle's room. With an energetic shake of Scrooge's hand, he addressed his patient in something less, though not much less, than a shout. "WELL, SIR, WHERE DOES IT HURT?"

Scrooge said he was not in pain.

"THEN WHY DID YOU SUMMON ME?"

Scrooge said it was his nephew who'd called him.

"WHAT'S WRONG WITH YOUR NEPHEW?"

Scrooge hoped nothing ailed his dear sister's boy.

"THEN AM I TO EXAMINE YOUR SISTER?"

Scrooge pointed out that his sister had been dead many years, and gave Dr. Hopkins a look that suggested he ought to have been acquainted with that fact.

"WELL, SIR, WHY THE DEUCE *AM* I HERE?"

Scrooge said he had not been sleeping well.

"WHEN A MAN GROWS OLDER, HIS BODY

REQUIRES LESS SLEEP."

Scrooge explained that it was not the quantity of slumber that was at issue, but the quality, or rather, the lack of it.

"WHAT DO YOU MEAN BY THAT?"

Scrooge explained that his sleep was disturbed by melancholy dreams.

"PERHAPS YOU HEAR ECHOES OF HEAVENLY TRUMPETS."

Scrooge allowed that he might.

"IT'S TO BE EXPECTED, SIR. NONE OF US LIVE FOREVER."

With that pithy observation, Dr. Hopkins prescribed a weak solution of opium in spirits and went away.

That night, just before bedtime, Scrooge dutifully swallowed his sleeping-draught and promptly laid himself down. In less than ten minutes, the laudanum took effect and he fell into a deep and blessedly dreamless slumber. A few such nights passed in undisturbed rest, and Scrooge's mood measurably brightened, for he thought he'd shaken his affliction for good and all, and so he told his nephew.

But the next night, though he retired early and took his medicine and swiftly fell asleep, Scrooge opened his eyes just before dawn and beheld a solemn Phantom, draped and hooded, coming like a mist towards him. The Spirit was shrouded in a deep black garment, which concealed its head, its face, its form, and left nothing of it visible save one outstretched hand. The very air the Spirit passed through seemed charged with mystery. It did not speak, but Scrooge knew its name.

The Ghost of Christmas Yet to Come.

Turning his head in the direction that the spectre pointed, Scrooge recognized the gate and front portal of his former lodgings. The door with its massive knocker gaped wide, but there was no light within.

Scrooge addressed the spectre. "Spirit, why show me this? I do not tread the path that once led me through that dark doorway."

It made no reply. The spectral hand pointed to the door.

"No, Spirit!" he protested. "I was promised three hauntings, and three hauntings is what I got. I've repented my miserly ways. Anything else you wish to show me is mere —" He pulled the pillow over his head and completed his remark with a muttered word that hadn't passed his lips in eleven years.

"— mere *humbug.*"

After a long silence, Scrooge peeped out from beneath the counterpane and saw that he was alone. He got out of bed, donned his dressing-gown, lit a candle and spent the rest of the night reading the Book of Revelation.

In the past eleven years, no sinner bowed his head or bent his knee with more heartfelt contrition; no voice sang the old hymns with more fervour; no worshipper attended sermons with greater concentration than Scrooge. Though he did not restrict himself to a single parish, but sought out chapels and cathedrals in every neighborhood of London, he had a favourite place of worship to which he often returned: the Church of St. Dismas, two blocks north of the Thames and just east of London Bridge. The sermons of Father Francis could always be counted upon to be comforting, so the morning after his waking vision, Scrooge left the house before Fred and his family were astir, and sought out his customary pew.

To his dismay, Father Francis was abed with the croup, and a visiting clergyman was officiating, instead. Scrooge's first impression of Father Macclesfield was less than favourable. He was a dry little man with a large hooked nose and sandy hair.

He began his sermon in an even, uninflected voice. "Last night, I dreamt of a mighty Spirit who traverses the world without pause or rest. It has no pity or compassion; it looks into the eyes of lions in their lairs, and they are dust; its shadow darkens hungry children, and they crave no further morsel.

"Now in my dream I saw a Minister of State. Round about him the cries of the ignorant and the poor pierced his heart, for he knew those who suffered most were the children of the land, so he proposed to the gentry that they devise some means to alleviate the people's sorrows. But the factions at court quarreled day and night and ended up doing nothing. And the Minister said, 'We must endure this great wrong in our time. Our successors shall cure it.' And all his court agreed, and put it from their minds.

"I watched in dread as the wrongs they ignored gathered into a dark poisonous mass that issued from the slums and penetrated to the highest places. The tainted breath of wretches breathing their last in deep cellars spread across the sky like smoke, and choked rich and poor alike. And still the Minister and his councillors shrugged and said, 'These wrongs will last out our time, and then shall pass away.'"

Father Macclesfield cleared his throat. "Then the mighty Spirit of my dream appeared before these gentry and the Minister of State, and asked them, 'How long shall *your* time last?'

"The Minister of State replied, 'My father died at eighty-four, my grandfather at ninety-two, thus I expect to be long-lived.' And the rest of the company reckoned one term, and some another, but each thought they would last longer than their three score and ten.

"'So each of you *is* allotted a time?' the Spirit asked, and every man exclaimed, 'Yes!' and then the Spirit, in a voice of thunder, said, 'This is true, and that time is ETERNITY.'"

Father Macclesfield's voice suddenly rose in volume; Ebenezer Scrooge sat straight up in his pew.

"'*Eternity*,' declared the Spirit, 'for whoever shall look upon a Great Wrong and take no action against it, that man shall bear his portion of that Great Wrong for ALL TIME!'

"And lo! the Spirit revealed its countenance, and all of them, preachers, gentry and the Minister himself looked upon the Angel of Death, and succumbed.

"Now when I woke," said Father Macclesfield, "I knew this vision to be true. For each of us who witnesseth a Great Wrong can never rest till it be set right. If we allow it to endure, the time of our bitter regret shall be . . . *forever!*"

Father Macclesfield raised his hands, delivered the benediction and spoke no more.

As the closing hymn died away, Ebenezer Scrooge left the church and headed south for the Thames embankment, where he proposed to stroll and ponder the priest's solemn words.

Despite the keen wind, he walked beside the river for nearly half an hour. Presently his energy flagged, and he sat upon a bench. In the distance, St. Dismas's chimes tolled noon. Scrooge shielded his eyes from the high October sun and stared out over the water.

"*Mr. Scrooge!*" A bright, eager voice disturbed his reverie.

Looking up, he saw a young man of medium height in black trousers and woolen overcoat. He clasped Scrooge's gloved fingers in the warmest of handshakes. Now custom had not inured Scrooge to such displays of gratitude; rather than pleasing him, they served as pointed reminders of the many opportunities he'd once wasted to help his fellow-men. On this present occasion he felt particularly unworthy of thanks, inasmuch as he could not name the youth who pumped his hand so enthusiastically. But as the wind blew with bone-chilling malevolency, and Scrooge clutched the collar of his topcoat, he suddenly recalled a child in a jacket too thin and worn to keep out the wintry blast.

"Is it possible?" He peered at him squint-eyed. "Are you the boy I met that Christmas? The lad whose mother was ill? Your name was — don't tell me . . . Paulie?"

The other smiled. "It's Paul. Mother still calls me Paulie."

"Is your mother —?" Scrooge hesitated. "Is she well?"

"Yes, thanks to you, Mr. Scrooge, she is indeed."

"The credit that day belonged to you, lad."

"Oh, no! you saved her, sir — and *me* as well."

"You? What did I save you from?"

"I nearly broke into the apothecary's shop to steal that worthless medicine of his."

Scrooge trembled; he recalled how his first close look at Paulie had reminded him of that angry, malnourished dream-child whose name, according to the Ghost of Christmas Present, was Want.

Paulie saw the old man shiver and misunderstood. "It's too cold out here, Mr. Scrooge. Have you had your mid-day meal? Mother would be delighted if you'd share it with us, and so would I!"

Scrooge said it would be inconsiderate to drop in unannounced, but Paulie laughed. "I could invite half the population of London at a moment's notice, and Mother would not mind. *Do* say you'll come!"

Warmed by the sincerity of the invitation, Scrooge agreed, so Paulie hailed a cab, and they rode off together.

Eleven years earlier, Ebenezer Scrooge had set up Paulie's mother as assistant manager at a millinery indebted to Scrooge & Marley. She and Paulie moved to a quiet block halfway between Bethnal Green and Victoria Park, a change that initially pleased but ultimately disturbed her, distancing her as it did from friends and near-neighbours. Some of them at least she saw Saturdays at the Great Synagogue in the East End, which she attended in preference to the new West London reform temple where Paulie wanted to go, but which she dismissed as "that place where the rabbi talks English; a church for Jews who want to be goyim!"

The cab pulled up in front of Paulie's home. Scrooge tried to pay the fare, but the youth would not hear of it. He ushered his guest up a short flight of stone steps, into a cozy, immaculate parlour. A tiny birdlike woman in a large white apron bustled into the room, fussing in sham distress and genuine pleasure.

"Pasey-Paulie, look who you brought! and the house *such a mess!*" Ida Cohen squeezed Scrooge so hard he was at once startled, embarrassed and pleased. "Please, Mr. Scrooge," she said in a breathless rush, "sit, make yourself at home, take off your shoes, relax."

"Thank you, madam, I *will* sit down."

"In my own home I am not called madam, to you I'm Ida."

"So be it. Ida, what was it you just called your son?"

"Sometimes," the youth replied, "she calls me Pasey-Paulie."

"Pasey," his mother explained, "is short for Pesach. That's when Paulie was born, on Pesach."

"Pesach means Passover, Mr. Scrooge."

"I know, lad. Passover occurs around the time of Easter. Don't be surprised. I used to do a considerable amount of business with your people."

Ida said, "Paulie once told me you had a Jewish partner."

"Indeed. When we first met, Jacob Marley was the son of an Austrian Jewish money-lender, but when he and I entered into partnership, he converted to Christianity."

She pursed her lips. "For personal or for business reasons, I wonder?" She brushed the question away. "It's none of my business. My business is fixing you a nice Jewish meal. I won't be a moment!" She scurried into the next room.

But it was a very long moment before the linen and dishes saved for special occasions were fetched, unfolded, dusted, washed, dried, arranged on the table. During these preparations, the guest of honour settled onto a worn horsehair sofa. His head lolled upon a white doily antimacassar; his chin rested on his bosom and he snored peacefully.

"It's a shame to wake him," Mrs. Cohen whispered.

"Mama, I found Mr. Scrooge sitting all alone by the Thames. Do you think he gave away all his money and he's homeless?"

"No, Paulie, look at his suit, such fine material! Still, as your dear Papa (God rest his soul!) used to say, 'there's poor and then there's *poor*.'"

Scrooge woke with a start. "Dear, dear, how rude of me!"

'Not at all," his hostess demurred, "I made you wait so long, no wonder you caught forty winks. Come, we'll have a few bites now."

Paulie escorted Scrooge into a dining room about the size of the mud room of his nephew's new home. Scrooge was not expecting much of a meal in a household of such modest means, but he was pleasantly surprised at the bounty of the Cohen table. Not that there was a great quantity of anything, but there were many plates and bowls, and Paulie identified their exotically unfamiliar contents, "bishkedeem," for instance, a flat-fish fried with slivered almonds and bananas; doughy pockets of hot potatoes and onions called "pierogies"; a plaited bread called "challah," and other morsels Scrooge more easily identified, though at the close of the meal when he praised the apple pie, he was told with great earnestness that there were no apples in it.

Scrooge tasted another forkful. "No apples? This is witchcraft!"

"Well," Ida laughed, "it *is* my mother-in-law's recipe. Now what can I get you, a nice cup of tea, or maybe you'd like another nap? You do look tired, Mr. Scrooge."

"I haven't been sleeping all that well."

A doleful click of her tongue. "*'Nur die Alten und die Bösen können schlafen nicht.'* That's what my mother used to say."

"What does it mean?"

"Only the old (you should pardon the expression), only the old and the wicked cannot sleep."

"Well, I'm certainly old enough," Scrooge admitted, "but I fear it must be some lingering wickedness."

"*You?* Wicked?"

"Mr. Scrooge," Paulie protested, 'you're God's angel on earth!"

"Hardly that, lad. The morning you first encountered me I was a changed man. Had you met me one

day earlier, you would have seen the most squeez-
ing, wrenching, grasping, scraping, clutching, covet-
ous old sinner in —" Scrooge was about to say "— in
Christendom," but opted instead for "the whole wide
world."

Ida marveled. "What miracle could bring about
such a change?"

"It *was* a miracle, though my nephew thinks it
was a dream."

"A dream?" Paulie echoed. "Tell us about it!"

"Pasey-Paulie! Mind your manners! He's a big
boy, Mr. Scrooge, but he's still got a little boy's curiosity."

"Curiosity is a fine trait. It would please me to
tell the tale of my spiritual redemption. My own
family has heard it so often that I have not related it
in some time, and like The Ancient Mariner, I have
need to tell it every now and again. It is only fair to
warn you, though, that it is a ghost story."

"In that case," Ida said, jumping up, "I'll go wash
the dishes. If I hear a ghost story, I wouldn't sleep
for two nights." She swooped down on the table like
a bird and began to snatch up crumbs. "Go, you two,
go to the other room and talk."

The men retired to the parlour. Scrooge settled
himself upon the horsehair sofa and began to tell his
story. "The day before the Christmas that we met,
lad, my nephew Fred visited my office and said
things that, though I was loath to admit it at the
time, started me thinking about my life . . ."

In spite of her intention not to listen, Ida Cohen could not help but overhear, and by the time Scrooge told about the school he sat in as a boy neglected by his father at Christmas, she abandoned all pretense of doing the dishes and joined her son in the parlour where she listened, spellbound, while Scrooge retold his tale with as much wonder as if it had just happened to him.

". . . and then I told Bob Cratchit, 'Stoke the fires, and buy another coal-scuttle before you dot one more *I*.' I bought him a splendid luncheon and set about helping him and his family, especially poor Tiny Tim, who did not die. And that's how I learned, my friends, that playing the Good Samaritan is one of life's greatest joys."

"Did the ghosts leave you alone after that?" Paulie asked.

"Years have come and gone without my seeing any other spirit — until last night when I was revisited by the Ghost of Christmas Yet to Come."

"Ach . . . now I *know* I won't sleep to-night!"

"Do you mean you dreamt of the ghost?" Paulie asked.

"It seemed as if I was wide awake. But whether it was a dream or no, something is troubling me, some deed of mercy, some act of charity undone."

"But you've become the soul of generosity," Ida argued.

"Surely," her son said, "the ponderous chain foretold by Marley's ghost has long since been un-

53

made."

Scrooge knit his fingers together, and sighed. "Too many years I hardened my heart to the woes of my fellow-men. Perhaps I have begun to substitute spiritual complacency for that earlier indifference. Who knows what necessary work I've left undone? If I were Catholic, I suppose I could rid this sense of obligation in the confessional, or if I were Jewish, I could attend that communal absolution that Jacob Marley once told me about." He noticed a glance pass between mother and son. "Did I just say something wrong?"

"*Kol Nidre* is what you're talking about," said Ida, "but what you're talking about is not *Kol Nidre*."

"I don't understand."

"Once a year," she said, "it's true that Jews pray to be released from pledges made during the preceding year."

"Isn't that what I said? Communal absolution."

"No, Mr. Scrooge," Paulie said, "not in the sense you mean it. The name of the prayer, *Kol Nidre*, means 'all our vows,' but it only refers to promises made to God." The young man clasped his hands and rocked gently, a mannerism he'd picked up from his father. "Let's say a banker's wife is suddenly taken ill. He promises that if God restores her to health, he'll donate one hundred pounds to the synagogue. Her sickness passes and she's well again, but his finances suffer a serious reversal and suddenly he can't afford his promise. At the next High Holiday services, he recites *Kol Nidre* and, provided he was sincere when he made the vow, he's released from it. After all, God doesn't need his money." Paulie's forefinger waggled. "But if this same banker promised one hundred pounds to the physician if his wife got better, he must pay it unless the doctor releases him from his promise. *Kol Nidre* applies to heavenly, not earthly obligations."

His mother beamed. "A mind and a mouth like a rabbi!"

"Mama, London doesn't need another rabbi."

"You do have a gift for words, lad," Scrooge observed.

"Maybe, but words alone can't put food on the table."

"But your mother did, and splendid food it was, too. My belly is full, lad, but you've also afforded me food for thought. No nobleman in all England has enjoyed better fare than I have this afternoon!"

Scrooge returned home just before six o'clock. His worried nephew asked where he'd been.

"To quote that old play, Fred, to-day was devoted to matters sad, high and working. Tomorrow, I must set out upon a journey."

"Where to?"

"To my past."

That evening when Scrooge went to bed, he decided to risk not taking his medicine. He slept till morning and the only dream he had was of the new sign high on the building over his office, but instead of SCROOGE, MARLEY & CRATCHIT, it said in letters of fire, *Whoever shall look upon a Great Wrong and take no action, that man shall bear his portion of that Great Wrong for ALL TIME!*

Stave Two

THE GHOSTS OF CHRISTMAS PAST

That great sinned-against sorcerer Prospero reminds us that we are such stuff as dreams are made on, but what are these airy fantasies that visit us at night? Humbug aftermaths of undigested beef, mustard, cheese, crumbs of underdone potato, or naked fragments of truth?

Scrooge's life was undoubtedly changed by the ghosts that haunted him, but was his haunting supernatural, or the workings of a rusty conscience stirred by a confluence of influences?: his nephew Fred's oratory, Bob Cratchit's miserable condition, the lad whose Yuletide carollings Scrooge squelched, the gentlemen whose charitable solicitations reminded the old man that Christmas was the anniversary of Jacob Marley's death.

Scrooge's family had often heard the tale of his miraculous conversion, but his nephew attributed the significant event to natural causes, partly because it happened in a single night, not over the course of three evenings as Marley's ghost had foretold.

One may therefore imagine Fred's state of mind when Scrooge, describing the vision he'd seen two nights earlier, exclaimed, "It was the Ghost of Christmas Yet to Come! Do you understand this portent?"

Fred sipped his tea. "I await your interpretation, uncle."

"I heard a sermon declaring that if we encounter injustice and take no measures to correct it, our immortal soul is in jeopardy. The Ghost of Christmas Yet to Come beckoned me to look back upon my old ways. What unfinished business is there for which I may yet be called to account?"

"You mean that business of dragging chains all through the Afterlife?"

"Not just chains, lad. Chains weighed down with cash-boxes, padlocks, ledgers, heavy purses wrought in steel. *I saw them*. One poor wretch I knew in life is required to traverse Eternity with a great iron safe attached to his ankle. But that's not the worst of it, it's travelling the cold streets of this world, everywhere witnessing mankind's suffering without being able to do anything to alleviate it — *that* is the true curse of the damned."

"A fine Christian sentiment, uncle, which just proves that your life has long been one of charity and compassion."

A vigorous shake of his head. "Father Macclesfield's sermon torments me, Freddie. '*Some great wrong.*' What business makes my soul so restless? Surely there is something I must make amends for. Therefore I must needs revisit those bygone places once shown to me by the Ghost of Christmas Past."

But Scrooge could not embark upon his homeward journey (as he regarded it) as promptly as he wished. First, there was the matter of hiring a suitable conveyance. While money was no object, still it took some casting-about before a coach-driver could be found agreeable to a junket for an unspecified period of time when the roads were likely to be difficult. Next there was the matter of travelling gear; Fred's wife refused to be appeased with the hasty inventory that the old man, in his haste to depart, intended to make do with. No, there were purchases to be made: scarves, gloves, a new hat and a thick coat were certainly necessary! Yet even taking these delays into account, Scrooge might have been on the road in less than a fortnight had his nephew not taken it into his head to arrange another appointment with Dr. Jack Hopkins.

"Uncle," he declared, "humour us. What if you fall ill in some remote place amongst strangers who do not know you have family in London?"

So Scrooge wearily submitted to another bout with the physician, who, after a great deal of prodding and poking, maintained that a trip such as he meant to undertake must be a risk to life and limb.

"HORSES SLIP SHOES AND BREAK LEGS," Dr. Hopkins warned. "WHERE WOULD YOU BE THEN, SIR? SHIVERING IN A STALLED COACH, OR TOSSED IN SOME MUDDY DITCH. AND WHAT OF COUNTRY INNS AND THEIR POORLY HEATED BED CHAMBERS? YOU'RE MORTAL, MR. SCROOGE, YOU ARE MORTAL!"

That fact, his patient quietly observed, had not altogether escaped his attention.

"THIS RISKY VENTURE MUST BE DELAYED TILL SPRING, WHEN THE ROADS, AT

LEAST, WILL BE IN BETTER SHAPE."

Fred seconded the doctor's opinion, but Scrooge declared he'd already delayed too long, and must set forth immediately.

"IF YOU INSIST ON THIS BUSINESS, AT LEAST DO NOT GO ALONE. TAKE A SENSIBLE COMPANION TO WATCH YOU AND PRESERVE YOUR CARCASS."

That suggestion somewhat reassured Fred and rather pleased Scrooge. Thereupon he sent a message to Ida Cohen, asking whether, for a stipend and incidental expenses, she would allow her son to accompany him on an excursion of several days duration. Ida discussed it with Simon Besserman, the tailor to whom the lad was unenthusiastically apprenticed. Besserman said the lad would do well to accommodate his family's erstwhile benefactor. This process added several days to Scrooge's already long-delayed departure, as did the old tailor's labours to make his apprentice a sturdy suit of black gabardine for the journey.

In the meantime, Scrooge's nephew visited the offices of Scrooge, Marley & Cratchit and held conference with its junior partner.

"Bob," said Fred, "are you acquainted with this young man my uncle intends to travel with?"

"Paul Cohen, you mean?"

"Yes. Is he reliable?"

Bob Cratchit smiled. "When he was nine years old, he did a service for Mr. Scrooge that greatly pleased my family."

"But isn't the lad —" Fred's brows contracted as he tried to think how to phrase his question. "Isn't he a . . . foreigner?"

Cratchit fidgeted. "Mr. Scrooge has spoken well of him."

"I'm sure he's a fine young man. But if my uncle must go on this pointless quest, I do wish he'd take someone with him more akin to himself in spirit and kind."

Bob smiled. "If I may make a suggestion . . . ?"

"Please do."

And so it came to pass that when Ebenezer Scrooge at last set out on a slate-grey day in late September, it was in the company of two fellow-travelers: Paulie and Bob Cratchit's son, Timothy.

The two instantly liked one another. Paulie took hold of the other's walking-stick, lent his shoulder, and returned the stick once Tim hauled himself into the carriage. Paulie got in and said, "You're Tiny Tim! Mr. Scrooge told me about you."

"And he told me about *you*. You're the boy who fetched us that great turkey —"

"'The one as big as me!'" They said it in unison, and laughed in unison.

"It's almost like being characters in a book," said Timothy.

"Except we're not the heroes!"

"*I* thought we were!"

"So did *I!*"

More merry laughter. When Ebenezer Scrooge joined them, they winked at one another in mock solemnity. Thus mirth signaled the beginning of their friendship, and that is perhaps the best way to enter the vestibule of that sacred institution.

Presently the coach got under way, and soon the great city vanished, and with it went its darkness. The horses trotted into a clear, cold autumn day with snow heaped up on the ground.

Scrooge, partly to fill the time and partly to calm his nerves, retold in small those great events he'd told before in large. "My nephew Fred believes it was all a dream," he remarked as they jounced and rattled along, "but I swear that it happened: Jacob Marley and all the other spirits. What do you think, lads?"

Timothy and Paulie discussed the question with the zestfulness of youth. Paulie was inclined to champion the rational explanation, while Tim leaned towards the miraculous. Each outlined his reasons, each perceived the worth of the other's arguments, each bent a bit. Thus ever should men of good will approach the heart's problems, old and new.

After much pleasant conversation and much unpleasant jouncing along roads whose snowy slipperiness required slow and steady progress, the old man decided they would all do well to get a good rest and resume their journey early upon the morrow. So at the earliest convenience, they stopped at an inn for the rest of the afternoon and evening. The next morning, after a hearty English breakfast, they set out in weather much like the day before. By that afternoon, Scrooge was able to look out of the carriage window and recognize the outskirts of a landscape familiar from his childhood years.

"How well I remember!" said Scrooge, clasping his hands together. "How well! I was born in this place. I was a boy here!"

As they rode along, he recollected every gate, and post, and tree. Shaggy ponies trotted by with boys upon their backs, who called to other boys in country gigs and carts, driven by farmers. All the lads were in great spirits, and shouted to each other, until the broad fields were so full of merry music, that the crisp air laughed to hear it.

Scrooge thought to himself, *They have no consciousness of us, they are hardly aware of their own consciousness, and that's how it should be. Time enough when they grow old to think upon the scant Time we mortals are apportioned.*

With one accord, as if they could read his thought, Timothy and Paulie clasped Scrooge's hands in theirs.

The first stop was a dilapidated schoolhouse, or, rather, the ruins of such an institution. They left the high-road by a well-remembered lane and approached a mansion of dull red brick, with a little weather-cock surmounting a cupola on the roof, and a bell hanging in it. It was a large house, but one of broken fortunes; its gates were decayed, its coach-houses and sheds were overrun with grass, its windows were broken, its walls damp and mossy with gaping holes in the plaster that showed the naked laths behind and let the weather leave its rude impressions upon woodwork and wallpaper, smearing them with patchy blisters and a distinctive taint of mildew.

Paulie and Timothy helped Scrooge out of the coach and followed him through the abandoned halls of the schoolhouse to a door at the back that, opening before them, disclosed a long bare melancholy room with one plain broken desk resting on its side near an empty fireplace, like a dunce relegated to punishment.

Not a latent echo in the house, not a squeak and scuffle from the mice behind the panelling, not a sigh in the leafless boughs of one despondent poplar in the dull yard behind, not the idle swinging of an empty storehouse door, no, not the clicking of a beetle in the dry fireplace, but fell upon Scrooge's ears with melancholy influence. With a shake of his head, he murmured, "Nothing but ghosts, nothing but ghosts." A long, frozen moment, then the old man turned and passed back out along the chilly passage to the front of the house.

The boys thought he was going to leave, but in the vestibule he turned left and passed through an archway into the shivery sanctum of an old chamber, where shrivelled tatters of maps on the walls were waxy with the cold.

"This once was the headmaster's best parlour," Scrooge said. "I had not thought it could become yet chillier than it once was."

"This was your school?" Paulie seemed oddly eager.

"This is where my father exiled me. After my mother died, my father grew cold and brusque. He spent his time doing accounts and collecting rents. I was an inconvenience, so he sent me here, and when Christmas came and all the other boys went home to their families, he did not call for me. Here I remained and celebrated the holiday with thin gruel and ill-stoked fireplaces in the company of my only friends . . . Ali Baba, Robinson Crusoe and other imaginary characters whose acquaintanceship I made in books I borrowed from the headmaster. I suppose he must be dead by now."

"But your sister rescued you at last, didn't she?" Tim prompted, knowing the answer.

"Yes, my nephew Fred's mother, little Fan. Her sweet nature mellowed my parent at last; it was she who prevailed upon him to send for me, it was she who finally brought me home."

"And was your father kinder to you then?" Tim asked.

"He was not unkind, just indifferent. Once only, he displayed mild approval on learning I had a head for business." For a long moment, Scrooge was silent, then, with creased forehead, he murmured, "Before I return to London, I must visit Fan's grave."

They drove down the garden-sweep of the old school; the wheels dashed the hoar-frost and snow off the dark leaves of the evergreens like spray. When dusk came on, the weary old man asked the coachman to put in at the first country inn he encountered. Presently, they rode up to an old gabled building with a sign that proclaimed it The Maypole. The landlord, a ponderous, slow-witted fellow, studied the party for several seconds with especial attention to Paulie, before declaring that he had no rooms. Scrooge gave the landlord a long, hard look before signalling the coachman to drive on.

They rode a while longer, tired, hungry, till at length the carriage clattered onto the thoroughfares of a market-town. They put in at the first inn they could find; the coachman took care of the horses, and Scrooge and his two young friends supped and went to bed. Though Scrooge fell asleep at once, his slumber was filled with dreams full of incident. He woke at sunrise, his body aching with the knocks and jounces endured in the ride from London.

Scrooge was filled with doubts. Was it too late to accomplish that nameless, neglected act of charity that troubled his rest? Was his past buried like the decaying relict of his old school?

The companions broke their fast with hearty country fare: eggs, pheasant, stewed tomatoes, beans, bread and beer. Paulie picked at his food; Tim encouraged him to a rasher of gammon, but when he declined, Scrooge summoned the landlord and asked him to fry up some kippers, "but not in lard."

"Thank you," said Paulie. "Where do we go today?"

The old man's tongue clicked against the roof of his mouth. "I'm almost afraid to say. I should have been better prepared for what I must find. The school in ruins — I should have known; why, it was already running to seed when I left it. What makes me think I'll find anything remaining of a life that began so many decades in the past? All things pass away."

Timothy exclaimed, "The love of God endures forever!"

"We hope it does," Paulie murmured.

Timothy heard. "Surely God's love is basic in every faith?"

"In our religion, we're encouraged to question everything, even God's existence. Not that my mother or most of the people I know would ever think of doing so."

"But what of the passage of Time?" asked Scrooge. "Do you remember any teachings concerning what it's like to grow old?"

Paulie reflected, then said, "There's a story my

father, may he rest in peace, told me when I was little. An old man returned to his boyhood home, and found nothing the same as he'd remembered it. He went to the rabbi, and said he was very sad that everything from his youth had changed. The rabbi, who was very wise, told the village folk to assemble in the town square. When they were all gathered there, he asked the old man to speak to the people.

"'But what shall I talk about?' he asked.

"And this was the rabbi's answer: 'Tell us what it was like when you grew up here. Spare no detail; speak of scenes and moments; make the time of your youth come again.' So the old man did, and children listened in wonder, and asked him many questions, and so did their parents, and afterward everyone thanked him for sharing his past because now they better understood their own. "And the rabbi said, 'They have seen the world as you saw it, and they rejoice. Now see it as they do, and rejoice. In this world both ephemeral and changeless, it is good to grow young as we grow old.'"

Scrooge looked at Paulie, then at Timothy, and smiled. "Doctor Hopkins was right. If it were not for the blessing of your companionship, I would not have the courage to proceed. But now I am prepared to go forth and seek out another fragment of my past."

"Where to?" both boys asked.

"If it's still there, I propose to visit the warehouse of that good old gentleman I was once apprenticed to ... "

"Old Fezziwig?!"

He nodded. "Old Fezziwig."

To their wonder and delight, the warehouse sign, though not fresh-painted, was still bright and legible:

FEZZIWIG & COMPANY
R. Wilkins, Proprietor

Scrooge was amazed. "Can it be? Poor Dick — perhaps he had a son?"

"Dick Wilkins?" Tim asked.

"Yes, my old friend. We were both apprentices to Fezziwig. Dick was sickly; I'd heard he'd passed away, but I was in London and never bothered to find out the particulars." Scrooge frowned. "It was soon after my dear sister died while giving birth to Fred. It was the beginning of that bleak period when I hardened my heart, but Timothy, you know about that. I am still ashamed that I, who was once a clerk myself, copying bills of lading and other dreary documents until my cramped hands could hardly move, that I should treat your poor father so wretchedly."

"He never spoke ill of you, Mr. Scrooge."

"Yes, I know, lad." He well remembered the glimpse the Ghost of Christmas Present had afforded him of the Cratchit Christmas, a detail he omitted when telling his history to the Cratchits. He knew Bob charitably refused to speak out against him, though Mrs. Cratchit was not so reticent.

The three entered the front office of Fezziwig and Company. A clerk in gaiters, long stockings and a vest, pushed a pair of spectacles up onto his forehead, wrinkled the latter, and inquired what their business might be. Scrooge explained he once worked for the firm, and hoped he might encounter someone dating back to that bygone time. The clerk ushered them into a capacious room at the rear of the warehouse, and told them to wait while he summoned Mr. Wilkins.

Paulie looked around the large chamber, openly amazed at the prospect. Any warehouse he'd seen in London was a study in dirt and squalour, but wherever he turned his eyes met gleaming fixtures and polished wood; even the most recondite corners displayed no trace of cobweb or dust-mote; scrubbed surfaces greeted him everywhere, and the strewn sawdust smelled sweet.

The door flung back on its hinges, and a slim, tall old man stepped into the room, arms wide, white whiskers flurrying. His smile was as broad as the Firth of Forth, his polished leather pumps almost tripping in his haste to catch Scrooge up in a hug that left both of them gasping.

"Ebenezer! Can it really be you?!"

"Dick Wilkins! Yes, dear Dick, yes, it's me, it's ME! But bless my soul, I thought you had passed away."

"Once I was near death's door, but that was long ago. Thanks to good old Mr. Fezziwig, I pulled through, and, as you see, managed to thrive. But I'd heard that *you* were dead!" He squeezed him in an even more ardent embrace.

"For far too many years, I walked the streets a living ghost." Scrooge laughed heartily. "But you'd best release me, Dick, these ribs are brittle with age."

Dick Wilkins ushered them into his office. Scrooge introduced his young companions to their host, who poured out four generous glasses of port. A round of toasts and a refill, and then the old men began to recount the events of the long years; like the worn sleave of a beloved coat that one cannot bear to part with, time unravelled and they clutched at the faded fabric of past events, places and people. And at length, as the boys knew he would, Scrooge told his story — *the* story — while his old friend listened, enrapt.

When the history of that haunted Christmas was over, Dick Wilkins declared it the most marvelous of mysteries. "Your story, Ebenezer, captures the Yuletide spirit, past, present and yet to come!"

"That's true," Timothy agreed, "though I think its power captures our heart and spirit because it reflects the infinite love of God for every one of us."

Smiling, Scrooge turned to Paulie. "Perhaps it means something else to you?"

Paulie's fingers lightly drummed his cheek.

"Christmas doesn't hold the same meaning for me that it does for you, Tim, yet Mr. Scrooge's story still moves me. I think I know why it captivates everyone who hears it, Christian or Jew."

"Tell us!" In his sweet, straightforward fashion, Tim had discerned that his new friend's spirit, like flintstone, was capable of illuminating sparks of new ideas, and lighting inner vistas that beckoned invitingly. "Tell us, *do!*"

Paulie stared at a spot on the ceiling, a habit he'd gotten into as a child when he learned that there was no place in a synagogue, not even the altar when the Torah was rolled open and read aloud by scholars, where he might see some image of God. He'd taken to looking up, high into the shadowy corners where darkness held both promise and emptiness.

"I think the story speaks to every human heart because it promises redemption, even in the last years of —" He stopped, but Scrooge patted his hand.

"You meant to say, even in the last years of a wasted life?"

"No, Mr. Scrooge, no!"

"Peace, lad, you would have put it differently, but that's the truth — that even an old, unscrupulous sinner like me was given a chance at the eleventh hour to save himself from —" He hesitated.

"From what?" Dick Wilkins inquired. "Hell-fire?"

"It's an odd thought. I was going to say an eleventh hour chance to save oneself ... from one's self."

Dick nodded. "Just as I said, Ebenezer."

In any meeting of those who share a past but have no common ground in the present, a time will come when conversation falters, and such a moment now befell our little gathering. Dick Wilkins bridged the gap by asking what had brought his old friend to revisit a town he'd long since quitted. Scrooge told him about his disturbing dreams, and how a sermon he'd heard led him to believe he'd neglected or overlooked "some Great Wrong that I must address and, if it is within my power, bring to rights. I set out on this journey, Dick, to see if there is something from my past that bears rectifying."

"I don't know if *this* qualifies," said Dick, fingers knit in an attitude almost like prayer, "but there's a great favour, Ebenezer, that your resources might enable you to perform for me."

Scrooge's eyes lit up. "Tell me!"

"I said earlier that long ago Fezziwig nursed me back to health, and in the main, that is true. I was sick unto death, and the rumour went abroad. Now Fezziwig's concern for me was shared by all the members of his household, but most particularly by his second eldest daughter Amanda. You remember her, don't you?"

"I recall her beaming smile."

"Ah, Ebenezer, it was her ministrations that ultimately restored me, her prayers on my behalf, her dainty hands guiding broth to my pale lips, her radiant spirit that led me by slow stages into the light. Of course I fell in love with her, and when I was on my feet again, I resolved to win her heart."

"It sounds to me as if you already had."

"Fezziwig knew that, and so did his wife, and so did his other daughters, but I was the last to find out. Recollect I was hardly a likely candidate, me just risen from the sick-bed and barely out of my apprenticeship, yet our dear employer sustained me and took me into the business as a junior clerk, with every hope of advancement. The following spring, Amanda and I were wed, and for a year and a day we lived blissfully."

He faltered in his narrative and with one finger brushed away the dew that welled up in deep-set blue eyes that, to Scrooge, retained much of the fire he possessed when both were young. The slim old man spoke again. "Amanda died giving birth to my daughter Martha, and, twenty years afterward, I weep to say, Martha met Our Maker in the same fashion, giving birth to my grandchild Amanda, whom I named in honour and memory of her grandmother, my beloved wife."

"And may I meet Amanda?"

"Ebenezer, I fervently hope you may, for that's the favour I beseech you to fulfill. About a year ago, my little Amanda met a rogue, an actor playing Romeo in a troupe that appeared here for a few days.

He worked his spell upon her, and when his company returned to London, she ran away with him."

"And have you heard from her since?"

"She wrote me once only." Dick Wilkins opened his desk, produced a folded missive and handed it to his friend.

Scrooge squinted at the address on the top of the letter. "Monmouth Street. I'm not familiar with it. Boys?"

Timothy did not know it, either, but Paulie did. "It's the East End, near the river. Lots of second-hand clothing shops."

Pursing his lips, Scrooge suppressed his opinion of the neighbourhood. "Dick," he said, "rest assured that I will seek her out as soon as we return to London."

"It won't be easy, Ebenezer." Dick's hand trembled as he took back the letter. "I wrote to her at this address, but it was returned. Amanda's moved, and I don't know where."

Many hugs, many proffered promises, many squeezings of the hand. Soon afterward, riding with the boys in their carriage, Scrooge happily declared, "This must be the deed I am charged to execute!"

"But are you sure, Mr. Scrooge?" Paulie asked. "You didn't even know that Mr. Wilkins was alive."

"That's exactly why I feel that this is what I must do! When I heard Dick had died, I barely took time to mourn him, and yet he was my friend. Now Fate has shown me how I may make amends for that omission."

"How will we find her?" Timothy asked. "London's so *big*!"

Scrooge replied, "We'll make inquiries at Monmouth Street. Why are you shaking your head, Paulie?"

"People in that quarter tend to be close-mouthed."

"A few pounds may open their lips."

"Are we returning to London now?" Timothy asked, a bit disappointed.

"We'll start back soon, but there's one more place I must visit. It is some distance from here and I must go there alone. You shall wait for me in town."

Nowhere in England is her antiquity more apparent than in her graveyards. Stones, grey stones blacking with coal-smoke, black stones green-grey with mosses come and gone, clay-red stones chipped and whittled by the wind, commemorative inscriptions no longer legible, mere ridges on the faces of the stones.

Scrooge's face might have been chiseled in granite. A sudden pinching of his lips as he noted the weeds and brambles grown around the grave, though he'd spent monies year after year, in spite of it being an unprofitable business to care for the upkeep of his sister's resting-place. But he blamed himself more than the grounds-keeper, for this was the first time Scrooge had returned to the cemetery since the new sod was turned over her coffin.

"Fan," he murmured, "I wouldn't blame you if you didn't recognize me after all this time. Forgive me for not coming back to see you. I couldn't." His voice grew husky. "Forgive me, too, for all the years I hardened my heart to your dear boy, Fred. I blamed him for your death — the same way Father banished me from his heart, though it was not my fault that Mother died. *Why* did Father hate me so?" Huskier still, and now the tears ran freely down Scrooge's cheeks, tears for old injustice that nothing afterward in life, not even money, can ever make up for.

Presently he grew calm. With considerable effort, he bent and picked up a pebble. He placed it on his sister's headstone.

"Fan, this is a custom my young friend Paulie told me about. His people place a small stone upon the grave of a loved one to show they've come and visited. A good custom . . . a stone for remembrance." He put a second pebble next to his. "And this one is for Fred, who's here with me in spirit. I've been good to him, Fan, I've made up for my old ways. He never asked me, though, for anything other than my love . . . the one thing that was hardest for me to give."

Scrooge was suddenly aware that someone's gaze had fallen upon him. A few rows of markers away, he perceived a gentleman of advanced years in a black greatcoat with a polished top hat in his gloved hand, a circumstance that enabled Scrooge to see that his observer had a generous head of salt-flecked pepper-black hair over a broad forehead, a generous mouth, and wide eyes that regarded him with a kind of perplexed look suggesting he was not certain whether he recognized the object of his scrutiny.

Scrooge brushed his hand against his sister's headstone in affectionate farewell, for he did not think it likely he would return to this spot until he was laid to rest beside her. Then he stepped across the intervening stretch of grass and greeted the gentleman in the black greatcoat.

"So it *is* you, Mr. Scrooge! We only met once, and that was quite some time ago. If you don't mind my saying so, you seem younger now than you did in those days."

"Thank you." Scrooge shook his hand. "You're Belle's husband, are you not?" Belle, the young woman to whom Scrooge was once betrothed, Belle, the beautiful friend and companion of his penniless beginnings, Belle, who gave him up unwillingly to the golden idol he'd begun to worship to the exclusion of every other human feeling, most particularly, love.

Belle's husband answered his question haltingly. "I — am."

"You live in London. You're far from home."

"So are you, Mr. Scrooge."

"My sister's buried here."

"Ah." The gentleman in the black greatcoat raised his hand and indicated the closest headstone. "You see why I am here."

Scrooge's heart froze. He remembered the pointing finger of the Spirit of Christmas Yet to Come, and the neglected grave with his own name written upon it, and he wished that it was that name that he was reading now, instead of Belle's.

"She came from these parts," her husband said. "She wanted to be buried here. Here, next to her father and mother."

"How long has she been gone?"

"Nine years to-day."

"I thought she was still alive." *Young, beautiful . . . Alive!* There at the close of her life, did she think of him and how he fell from grace? Perhaps she speculated on what star was destined for her habitation when her life had run its little course; perhaps she marvelled how the stars could gaze down on that perfidious creature, man, and not sicken and turn as green as chemists' lamps . . .

Belle's widower rested a consoling hand on his arm. "Mr. Scrooge, she still lives in our memories and in our hearts." He paused. "And something more . . ."

"Please tell me."

"Belle never stopped loving you, you know."

Scrooge cast down his eyes and examined with minute interest the brown muddy streaks of cemetery earth newly caked upon his shoes. "It's good of you to tell me that." Scrooge's eyes reflected pain that cannot be described, only felt. "Tombstones and tombstones, and yet the world runs on, uncaring. How could you endure so great a loss?"

"My children have sustained me in my grief. Their mother's spirit lives in them. Our oldest daughter is very like Belle. Mr. Scrooge, love sustains us all. What other reason are we put here for?"

Scrooge remembered his nephew's daughter, Fan, so like the grandmother she never knew. The breaking light of a thought: "Children . . . one's own children . . . must be such a blessing!"

"They are, Mr. Scrooge, they are."

"Where are your children now?"

"Back at the inn. I wanted a moment alone with Belle, my own private moment." On impulse, he squeezed the old man's arm gently. "Do you know, I would be delighted if you would come visit me and my family when we're both back in town. Do come some Sunday for dinner, it's such a festive occasion in our home."

"I should be honoured, sir!"

They shook hands and said farewell, but as the other gentleman turned to leave the cemetery, Scrooge lagged behind long enough to place a stone upon Belle's grave and whisper her name and utter three brief words.

In the carriage that evening, Scrooge did not speak for a long time. He stared out the window at the dying sun. Suddenly, he addressed Paulie.

"Lad, do you like working for Mr. Besserman?"

Paulie thought about it. "He's always been good to mother and me."

"I didn't ask you that."

"Tailoring's an honest trade," Paulie parroted.

"But have you never thought of something more? A higher education?"

"Mr. Scrooge, I'm Jewish — there's no school in all of England that would accept me."

"But emancipation is no longer an issue!" Tim exclaimed. "Baron Rothschild entered Parliament three years ago."

Paulie sighed. "Would that I were a Rothschild."

"Isn't there a movement afoot to start a Jewish college?"

"Yes, Tim, there's talk of it," said Paulie. "Charlotte Montefiore expressed open regret at the lack of Jewish culture, but no funds of any significance have been appropriated."

Scrooge listened to this exchange with keen interest, but kept his own counsel for the rest of the ride. Presently, the coachman reined in the horses, stopped the carriage, got down from his perch and said, "Here's a inn. I suggests we stop here, there's none other for miles."

Scrooge got out, but when he saw the sign of The Maypole, he shook his head. "This is the place that refused to give my young friend a room. We shan't stop here."

"We got to," the coachman grunted. "Hosses are done in, they needs fed, they needs sleep, and so does I."

"It's all right, Mr. Scrooge," Paulie said, emerging. "Maybe they'll let me stay in the stable with the horses. A stable seems appropriate, it's not that long till Christmas."

"If *you* have to sleep there," Timothy declared, also disembarking, "I will, too!"

"No one is sleeping in the stable," Scrooge said emphatically. "It's too cold, and even if it weren't, it's wrong! I'll speak to the innkeeper, and see what a few solid British pounds can't accomplish."

As Scrooge expected, the landlord could hardly resist double-rent, and grudgingly agreed to allow Paulie and Timothy to share a room, provided that the former take his meals therein and not set foot in the tap-room.

"Very well," said Scrooge. "Sir, I am curious about this inn. It is an interesting edifice. I would venture to say that it has seen its share of history."

"Fair to say that it's seen its share of years."

"And are you the proprietor?"

The innkeeper snorted. "Maybe if I live to be a hundred and fifty, that's how long it'd take me to pay off the mortage."

"I see," said the old man.

Later, Scrooge turned down the covers of a lumpy bed and reflected on the events of the day. *I'll find her. With Tim and Paulie's help, I'll restore Amanda Wilkins to her father. And as for my young friend, we'll see what can be done for him.*

Scrooge snuffed out the candle by his bed and shut his eyes, but could not slow his racing thoughts, so eager was he to return to London and set his designs into motion.

When at last he slumbered, he dreamed he lay in a dark, confined space with the rattling sound of stones raining down upon the lid of his coffin.

Stave Three

CHRISTMAS YET TO COME

Business, be its nature temporal or metaphysical, may march upwards or slide inexorably downward in the first ten months of the year, but November is a time for taking stock: and those bluff and blowzy with success grow another pound or ten fatter, and those impoverished in flesh or spirit suck in their cheeks and draw in their actual and metaphorical belts another notch tighter.

London in November. Nowhere is the leaf more sere, the wind more biting, the fog thicker, the daylight feebler (if it comes out at all); the sooty bricks and paving-stones slippery with mud beneath the plodding feet of chestnut-vendors and hot potato men hoarsely crying their wares as they slog through the smoke and grime of a great (and dirty) city.

Scrooge's spirit caught the weather, and his body caught cold. He spent his days at home snuffling, wheezing, resting with difficulty and spooning thick grey gruel into thin, blue lips. Elsewhere, Bob Cratchit did what he could to further his senior partner's intentions, and so did the boys.

On their way to Monmouth Street, Paulie pointed out a strange new spectacle to his friend.

"That's the old synagogue. The new one is in the West End."

"Which do you belong to?"

"This one. I'd rather go to the other, though even if my clothes were good enough, my mother would still object."

"Why?"

"Partly loyalty to the old neighbourhood. Partly because the West End temple uses English, not just Hebrew, in their services, and that's something she won't accept."

"But you would?"

"Absolutely. My mother thinks of herself as Jewish, and there's an end of the discussion, but I also think of myself as English."

Timothy gestured toward the synagogue's front entrance. "Would it be all right if we went inside?"

"You'll get an odd stare or two, but nobody will mind. Come on." Paulie guided him up the steps, through a foyer and into a dim chamber with a raised platform in the middle of it. "That's the *bimah*, that dais, where we read the Torah."

"What's the Torah?"

"Parts of the Bible. Old Testament stories, ethical principles, all written in Hebrew on rolled-up scrolls."

"Can you speak Hebrew?"

"Enough to get by. There's not much need to, not since we moved out of the old neighbourhood. Have you seen enough?"

Perhaps it was the dark, lofty ceiling and the up-slanted wooden rafters supporting the roof, perhaps the time-smudged walls streaked with the accumulations of London rains, but something about the synagogue fascinated Tim. He would have liked to stay longer, the place was so different, yet oddly familiar; its holiness comforted him. He wanted to take it all in, but Paulie clearly wanted to leave, so Timothy followed his companion out.

"Next stop," said Paulie, "Monmouth Street."

Now according to a popular author, Monmouth Street was once an important market for second-hand clothing. Its denizens shut themselves up during daylight hours in dark parlours and cellars, but there were still enough shifty-eyed peddlers and ragtag street urchins about to prompt both boys to keep their hands pressed against their wallets as they threaded their way through the tangled warp and woof of that colourful tapestry called London.

The address in Dick Wilkins's letter brought them to a dingy alley. They rapped at the grey door of an old tenement pockmarked with grey patches where the paint had peeled off its weather-beaten sides. They waited, knocked a second time, waited and tried yet again. They had just about decided there was no one within when the knob trembled, and the door opened to reveal a woman as grey as the portal itself. The sunlight was harsh on her face and her house; both were flaked with dried paint.

"A bit early, laddies. Coom back when t' lamps is lit."

Timothy's face reddened. Paulie steadied him and said, "We're looking for Amanda Wilkins."

"Nae, there's Alice, Elizabeth, Mary. Nowt Amanda."

"She lived here once." Tim held the letter out for her to read, but she would not take it.

"Daylight is fierce on me peepers. Read it, if y' will."

Realizing she must be illiterate, he read the letter aloud. The woman listened carefully; when the message was finished, she made a clucking sound and held up a lacquered fingernail.

"Och, wee Mandy, that's who ye mean. Dinna look sae doour, lad, coom in." With a jerk of her head, she led them inside to a tatty parlour. There was a scrappy horsehair sofa set against one grey wall and a plain deal table that wobbled as she sat by it. "Does ye've got a tot of whusky?"

"No," said Paulie, peeling off a pound note from a bundle Scrooge had given him, "but this is yours if you can help us."

She made no move to take it. "I dinna ask tha' in t' proofit. I tells meself, Bridey, these fine yooung laddies coom to help wee Mandy, who's in sair need o' help." She sucked her lips. "But all this talk sae early mus' be lubrified, me pipes are roosty."

This difficulty was resolved by dispatching a slipshod girl named Betsy with the pound-note to a nearby spirits shop. They waited in awkward silence till Betsy returned with a package in plain brown paper wrapping, and Bridey opened it and measured out a double portion of whisky that she worked in her mouth for several seconds before nodding that she was ready now for social interchange.

Paulie said, "We were told that Amanda met an actor she took a fancy to, and followed him to London."

"Aye, she was drupped off heer by that yooung rascal what thinks hisself better than he is: Bartie — Christian name, Bart'olomew."

Tim asked, "You know him then?"

"I du, though proud I'm not t' say it." She poured herself another drink. "He's m' son."

The two boys digested this news in silence, then Paulie asked if she knew where Amanda had moved.

Bridey shook her head. "I tried to keep 'er heer, but she wouldna stay. An' her in sooch a state . . ."

Meanwhile, in a parlour of markedly different character, Scrooge's nephew stared at his uncle in frank astonishment.

"Perhaps," said Fred, "I misunderstood you. You are thinking of doing — *what?*"

"You heard me right, m'lad. I would like to adopt Paulie."

"But doesn't he already have a perfectly healthy mother?"

"That he does. She is a dear, dear lady."

His nephew's eyes might have passed for saucers. "Uncle, you are not trying to tell me that you wish to marry this woman?"

Scrooge uttered a startled laugh, then stared at Fred as if he'd suddenly taken leave of his senses. "Good heavens, no! I have *not* fallen victim to that affliction that infects some gentlemen of advanced years. Ida Cohen is a fine woman, but where her son Paulie is concerned, she is of limited vision."

"I cannot hope to fathom your motive in this business."

"My motive, dear boy, is to ensure that a young man of promise is educated and trained to fill a loftier role in life than the tailoring trade to which he is apprenticed."

"Have you broached this plan to the boy and his mother?"

"In good time, nephew. That favour due my friend Dick Wilkins must take precedence, but hearken! I hear my scouts in the hallway. Timothy! Paulie! Come in here!"

The young men entered. Scrooge waved them to chairs at a table furnished with delectables and, clasping his hands together, listened as they described their sojourn to Monmouth Street. When they were done, he shook his head. "Tsk-tsk, so the poor girl's situation is desperate. You must find her, boys!"

"Bridey was hoping she'd changed her mind by now and gone back home," said Timothy. "She was sad to learn that she hasn't."

"Where do we begin to look for her?" Paulie asked.

Scrooge buttered a bun and thought about it. "You must search for that scoundrel Bartholomew. He's an actor, and that's a public profession. It shouldn't be difficult to track him down. Amanda may be close by, or he may know something of her whereabouts."

"If this Bartie's as unpleasant as his own mother says he is," Paulie observed, "I doubt that he'll answer our questions."

"He's an actor," said Scrooge, eating his buttered bun. "He earns his living posturing in public, assuredly a meager living. A few shillings ought to prompt the dialogue we wish him to utter."

While the three were thus engaged in tea-table strategy, Scrooge's nephew excused himself and left the house. He hailed a cab and rode to St. Bartholomew's, where he arranged for a private consultation with Dr. Jack Hopkins.

"Doctor H.," said he, "I confess that I and my wife are quite concerned about my uncle."

Dr. Hopkins asked whether Mr. Scrooge was still having difficulty sleeping.

"That's no longer the problem," Fred said, and proceeded to outline Scrooge's proposition to adopt a boy who was not only nearly grown up, but had already been furnished by Providence with a fully functional parent of his own.

Dr. Hopkins frequently punctuated this history with nods, knowing winks and portentous throat-clearings. When the tale was done, he promised to stop by before the week was out and render his professional opinion on the sensitive issue Fred had anxiously broached: that of Ebenezer Scrooge's mental competency.

Comfort is a commodity rarely associated with London dinner parties; it is generally subjugated to the traditions of etiquette and protocol, the niceties of formal attire, the intricacies of place and pomp, the prescribed formulae of cuisine taken neat with wines decanted below stairs by that stratum of society to which those overhead give scant thought, so long as they perform their duties without compromise or default.

But none of these routines, nor the customary conversational gambits taken in correct admixture with discussions of the Court Circular, nor that obligatory separation of the sexes so that gentlemen might partake of brandy and cigars; not one of these hallowed ceremonials were observed on that Sunday afternoon in November when Scrooge accepted the hospitality (and excellent dinner) of the widower of his long-deceased friend, Belle.

A large, attractive, laughing company seated round a large, attractive, groaning table. Service was prompt, yet no servants were to be seen; children and grandchildren with no thought of rank or precedence carried plates to and from the kitchen to an old mahogany sideboard, and from that sideboard to an old mahogany dinner table whose scratched, but polished surface supported such a remarkable selection and quantity of good food that Scrooge suspected his presence had prompted his host to incur far greater expense than would have been customary or prudent for a dinner so close in proximity to the upcoming Christmas feast.

Lively supper sounds dinned: the clatter of cutlery, the chink-chink of plates, the bright crystal ting of glassware touching other tumblers in convivial toasts, the happy chatter of jocular endearments and bursts of wit that produced laughter sufficient to undercut the pride of every overweening demon from St. Paul's Cathedral to St. Gavon's Monastery-in-the-South.

Scrooge weathered the festivities with mixed emotions. He was pleased to perceive the consequences of a life successfully accomplished in spite of limited means, yet he was also sad because it was one that he might have lived with all the abundant benefits of the love that he witnessed all about him now.

As the evening waned, and most of Belle's descendants dispersed to their own respective homes, Scrooge reflected that the Ghost of Christmas Past had once brought him, cloaked by invisibility, to a certain room neither large nor handsome but full of comfort, and here he was again in that very chamber holding quiet converse with his host and his middle-aged daughter Anna. She sat next to her own child, a maiden of sixteen years who bore both the name and beloved features of her late grandmother Belle.

"It is remarkable," said Scrooge, "how both of these ladies resemble Belle at different stages of her life." And he was right, for Anna and young Belle differed only so much as snow-flakes work changes on the same beautiful patterns of Nature.

"It is quite as remarkable," Scrooge's host replied, "how different you are from that shuttered spirit you once were. I do not intend to give offence."

"None is taken," said Scrooge. "Tell me, can you recall the last time but one that you set eyes upon me?"

Furrowed brows. "That's very long ago."

"Eighteen years ago, this Christmas," Scrooge nodded. "It was the night my friend and partner Jacob Marley lay dying."

The sussuration of a sharp in-drawn breath. "I remember! I passed by your office window. The room was lit by a single candle, and you sat there, all alone. I hadn't thought you'd noticed me."

"I didn't."

"Eh? Then how do you know I saw you?"

Scrooge immediately regretted his candour. The history of his Yuletide conversion was familiar (if doubted) within his own family circle, but to explain now that on a bygone occasion, a ghost had guided him to this very room where he had heard the dialogue concerning himself, surely would prompt his host to regard Scrooge as a daft old coot, or, if credited as truthful, as a presumptuous supernatural trespasser. Therefore, altogether ignoring his host's question, Scrooge said, "How heartless you must have thought me that night, carrying on my business of pounds and shillings when my sole remaining friend on earth lay alone, breathing his last tormented breath."

Belle's widower shook his head, but it was his daughter who spoke, instead. "I remember that night well, Mr. Scrooge, that Christmas Eve when Father came home and said he saw you sitting there all by yourself in your office."

"How could you, Anna?" her father asked. "You were just a little girl!"

"I was old enough, Father. I can still picture it ever so clearly. You told Mama you'd seen an old friend of hers that afternoon, and you asked her to guess who it was, and she knew right away it was Mr. Scrooge. Mama laughed —"

Too well, Scrooge thought, *too well* he recollected Belle's laughter that haunted night when, responding to her mate's invitation to guess which old friend he'd seen, she said, "How can I? Tut, don't I know?" and laughed, "Mr. Scrooge." And then Scrooge remembered his host saying to Belle that, with his partner Jacob Marley dying, Scrooge would be "quite alone in the world, I do believe," and that was when Scrooge had brokenly petitioned the Ghost of Christmas Past: "Spirit! remove me from this place. Remove me! *I cannot bear it!*"

All these painful thoughts raced through his mind in that scant second Belle's daughter paused for breath. "Ah, Father," she cried, "Mother laughed at first — but afterward, when you told her you thought Mr. Scrooge was now all alone in the world, how can I forget how bitterly she wept?!"

Belle shed tears for me?

"I hope I am not being presumptuous, Mr. Scrooge," said Anna, "but it is my belief that when you sat there doing business as your friend lay dying, you were not being heartless. I think it was the only way you could cope with a loss so great, you who had already lost so much . . ."

Scrooge pinched his nostrils with thumb and forefinger, and, fishing for a handkerchief, mumbled something about sniffles that he could not get quit of.

For the first time since the Ghost of Christmas Past had shown him what his worship of (as Belle put it) the "golden idol" had cost him, now for the first time Ebenezer Scrooge fully felt the weight of that death-in-life he had carved for himself that day when Belle, herself in mourning for the passing of her father, sadly released her fiancé from the nuptial contract they'd made when they were young and poor, and content to be so.

Is this what has been giving me nightmares? It was indeed a Great Wrong, but Belle had recovered from it, whereas Scrooge could never redress his own grief. He reflected on the pangs of lost love, and what an apt preparation it was for the heavy chains he still might shoulder in Purgatory.

A rustle of dainty skirts; Belle's young grandchild Belle, who'd sat quietly beside Anna, her mother, all the while, on an impulse, rose and knelt beside Scrooge. She clasped his hand in hers, and impulsively kissed his fingers. Scrooge patted her head and shut his streaming eyes and thought back to another time . . .

November passed by slowly, as it generally does. Why this should be so is at the very least, mysterious; November's tally, after all, is one day shorter than its near neighbours, and the very length of its days is curtailed by a long twilight that whittles down the month's thirty constituent members. But for whatever indefinable reason, the month crept by, and, copying its pace (or rather, the lack of it), Scrooge's schemes, if they may be poetically permitted to have feet, certainly dragged them.

The tasks he'd assigned Bob Cratchit were diligently undertaken, but as is often the case when one is in haste, all that might conspire to bring about delay came to pass.

Paulie and Timothy, meanwhile, put innumerable questions to that garrulous species known as show-folk, and received such a quantity of colourful and well-pronounced replies as might fill a folio in The Bodleian, yet nothing that they learned enabled them to set themselves upon the trail of Miss Amanda Wilkins or her seducer, Bartholomew MacGregor.

Dr. Hopkins at least made good on his promise to stop by and observe his patient, but other than a moist, lingering cough, that worthy found nothing odd that he judged worth reporting to Fred.

And then it was December.

On a wet Tuesday in the first week of the new month, early in the morning, a coach rattled into the City bearing several passengers, one of them a ponderous man of sixty furnished with a rising belly-mound, a collection of double-chins, and a frown as weighty as himself.

His scowl was bestowed upon the filthy streets and the foot-pedestrians who frequented the same: those raffish fellows who, upon a country road, might be taken for highwaymen (perhaps accurately); those beggarly children whose angelic mien masked their deftness at snatch-pursing and thievery; worst of all (a conclusion based upon the traveller's deepening disdainful glower), those grizzle-bearded, sharp-eyed, grasping scoundrels who pretended to be Englishmen, but whose true allegiance was reserved for countries and customs baked by a harsher, dryer sun.

The carriage came to a halt. The passengers got down and took their luggage. The fat man, hailed by name, was guided to a hackney coach, and whisked off. In less than fifteen minutes, he found himself standing, with wisps of steam curling about his boots, before the offices of Scrooge, Marley & Cratchit.

A puff of white vapour that was his breath preceded him as he stepped into a simple room dominated by a large, cheery fireplace that had been ordered eleven years earlier by the firm's senior partner as a special Christmas gift for the man who later became his junior partner.

"Mr. Willet?" a woman asked.

His thick neck turned. There were two others in the room with him, a gentleman of sufficient years, and a diminutive woman who repeated his name with an odd inflection that he immediately consigned to a mental compartment labelled Not English.

"Mr. Willet?" she repeated.

He looked down at her, figuratively and literally, and addressed, instead, the man. "Are you Mr. Scrooge?"

"I'm Mr. Scrooge's partner."

"You're Marley, then?"

"Mr. Marley has been dead these eighteen years. I'm Bob Cratchit. This is Mrs. Cohen. Kindly step into my office."

Grumbling that his business was with Scrooge, Willet did as he was told. Bob waited for Ida to be seated, then waved the visitor to a chair, sat at his desk and opened a large folder, extracting from it a sheaf of legal-sized papers bound together at the top. "Am I correct in assuming that you are Wilbur Willet, proprietor of the inn known as The Maypole?"

"Eigh. Trace us both, Maypole and Willet, that'll put you back to the late King Hal, maybe summat before that."

"*Tch-tch*." Ida's tongue clucked against the roof of her mouth. "All that time, and the business is *still* mortgaged?"

"That's my business, none o' your'n!"

"And what happened this month when you went to pay your rent?"

Willet glared at her. "They wouldn't take it. They said I had to go to London if I didn't want to lose The Maypole. At least they paid the coachman. But I'm here now, and I don't like it!?"

Bob Cratchit pushed the papers forward so Wilbur Willet could read them. "Upon the first day of this month, Mr. Scrooge discharged, and thus acquired, the mortgage from your creditors. I show you a record of that transaction. The hostelry known as The Maypole is now the sole property of Scrooge, Marley and Cratchit."

"So now I pay you instead o' the bank?"

"That is correct, sir."

The innkeeper exhaled a quart of air. "Couldn't they have told me that, and saved me a long, bone-rattlin' ride?"

"I am afraid not, sir. You see, Mr. Scrooge stayed at The Maypole a little while back, and he was not pleased with the manner in which you run the place."

The stout landlord lumbered to his feet, chins all a-quiver. "And is this Mr. Scrooge now planning to tell me how to run The Maypole?!"

"No," said Ida Cohen, "he hired me to do that —"

Had a witness noticed Mr. Wilbur Willet as he entered the offices of Scrooge, Marley & Cratchit that morning, that same observer must have wondered at the fat landlord's reduced substance when he quitted those same premises an hour afterward.

Unlike its laggard neighbour, December is inclined to hurry. A quickening of activity in shops: parcels wrapped up in brightly-coloured paper, caps in pink ribbons, pen-knives purchased, sweetmeats savoured and consumed; poulterers hanging great geese in their front windows; punch bowls and matching cups polished up in parlours private and public; decanters dusted, corkscrews secured, mistletoe plucked and hung; recipes for plum-cake and mince-pies newly consulted; and, most wonderful of all, as befits the beneficent promise of the season, all petty discords and jealousies brushed aside in a blizzard of invitations to kin-folk gathered in once more to the collective bosoms of their families.

Yuletide preparations, anticipated with great zeal, were undertaken with less bustle than usual in the household of Scrooge's nephew, for the old man's cold had not improved, and his slumbers, though undisturbed by further nightmares, were still fitful and restive. Dr. Hopkins suggested that he stay warm, and rest as much as possible, so Scrooge confined himself chiefly to his bed, where he swathed himself in night-cap, dressing gown and slippers. There, periodically breathing steamy vapours that afforded him some relief from congestion that made his head feel stuffed with cotton-wool, the old man busied himself reading reports and correspondences brought to him by Bob Cratchit.

But on the morning after Mr. Wilbur Willet visited his office, Scrooge dressed himself and descended to the parlour, where Paulie's mother sat sipping sherry while his nephew stood awkwardly in the hall in the company of Dr. Jack Hopkins.

Scrooge bowed to his guest. "Thank you for coming to see me, Ida. I regret any inconvenience I may have caused you. I have a mild case of grippe, but Dr. Hopkins insists on treating me as though I carried the plague."

"CAUTION IS THE BEST MEDICINE, SIR! IF YOU DON'T CONSERVE YOUR STRENGTH, YOU WON'T LIVE TO SEE ANOTHER CHRISTMAS!"

Scrooge leaned close to Ida. "He addresses me as if I were a deaf child." He straightened and spoke louder. "Gentlemen, I want you to hear and witness what I have to say to Mrs. Cohen."

Fred traded a glance with the physician, which Scrooge noticed with sour amusement. "Come now, don't hover about like spectres haunting the hall, sit down and hear what I have to say."

They entered the parlour. Fred chose a plain wooden chair opposite his uncle. Dr. Hopkins strode to the fireplace, where he studied his patient with crossed arms and a good-humoured twinkle.

"I am aware, Freddie," said Scrooge, "that you are afraid that I might be taking leave of my senses."

"Uncle, no!"

"Nephew, yes! To this day, you still believe that I only dreamed the three Christmas spirits, isn't that true, sir?"

Fred replied diplomatically. "It happened on Christmas Eve. I believe in all mysteries that derive from that great event."

"WELL SPOKEN, SIR!"

Scrooge smiled. "I know you had my best interests at heart when you consulted Dr. Hopkins after I divulged to you that business I mean to propose to this lady."

Ida, undaunted by the chamber's elegance, had been pleased to wait patiently to hear whatever her family's benefactor meant to impart. Now she sat up straight, her interest piqued.

"Madam," Scrooge began, but she waggled a finger at him and went *tch-tch*, so he emended his form of address. "Ida, you are aware that I hold your son in the greatest esteem."

"I know, and I'm grateful."

Scrooge acknowledged her thanks. "All philanthropists are aware that every act of charity is subject to the reinterpretation and sometimes the misinterpretation of disinterested parties, not all of whom are as charitable as the deeds they undertake to judge. Therefore, I wish to make it clear before these witnesses that nothing I have done for you or for Paulie now or in the past has ever carried any kind of price-tag."

"Who says different?!" she asked, raising her chin.

"To the best of my knowledge, no one. I voice the sentiment merely to set it aside, for I am about to propose something that I hope you won't regard as presumptuous. I have called you here to talk about Paulie's future."

Ida was surprised. "But that's the last thing you should worry about. He's going to make a decent living. He wouldn't ever sleep in a place like this, but he's clever and he works hard."

"Oh, Ida, Paulie is such an intelligent young man. Wouldn't you prefer something better for him than spending his life as a tailor?"

Ida stared into her wine-glass. "I wish I could look into the future the way I can look into this crystal and see wonderful things ahead, but I can't. If his father, God rest his soul, had lived, Paulie might study to be a rabbi, but things worked out the way they did, and that's that."

"Not necessarily. You know I have the means to help him. Would you permit me to finance Paulie's higher education?"

"Where could you send him? For rich Jews, yes, there has been a little progress in England in the past few years, but even for them, it's not so much. With all your money, Mr. Scrooge, you could never get him into Oxford or Cambridge or any decent school, and even if you could, it'd be a lot worse, believe you me, than staying for a night at The Maypole Inn."

"How did that go, by the way?"

She set down her empty glass. "That tub of lard will do what I tell him. The Maypole is his whole world, he won't risk losing it. It's good you rapped his knuckles, but he'll never change."

Scrooge gestured to the decanter, but Ida smiled and shook her head. "Thank you, no, another glass of wine and my head will go spinning around like a wheel."

"To return to the question," said Scrooge, "there is truth in what you say, but I have been giving this a great deal of thought, and I perceive a way that Paulie might attain the education he deserves."

"And what way would that be?" She sounded skeptical.

"I've asked my partner Bob Cratchit to research

the legal steps required for me to adopt Paulie as my son."

Ida's eyes goggled. She almost told Scrooge he was crazy, but, remembering Dr. Hopkins, restrained herself.

Scrooge continued. "You understand I mean this purely as a legal fiction. Sometimes in business it is necessary to take unusual measures. If he had papers to prove he was my son, Paulie — Paul would be accepted unchallenged at England's best schools." He turned to his nephew. "You see, Freddie, I've not progressed so far into senility as you feared. Do you agree, Doctor?"

"YOU'RE WILY AS A FOX, SIR!"

"I trust that opinion will serve to keep the alienist from my door." He stopped. "Ida, why are you shaking your head so vigorously?"

"Mr. Scrooge, you've always been very good to us, but what you're suggesting is out of the question. You've got a good heart, and it's wonderful that you should care so much for my Paulie. There are times when I think he would have been happy to call you father . . . grandfather, at least. Now don't be offended —"

Scrooge chuckled. "I accept the full weight of my years. But Ida, be reasonable. I don't think the law would permit me to adopt him as my grandson. Please tell me why my plan won't work."

She uttered a weary sigh. "How do I explain in a minute what it is to be an outsider all your life? How did your partner feel?"

"My partner?" The question perplexed Scrooge, then he realized that she was not referring to Bob Cratchit. "You mean Jacob Marley?"

"Yes. How did he feel when he converted?"

"As far as I could tell, he was perfectly content."

"*When* did he convert to Christianity?"

"When he and I —" Scrooge faltered. "When Jacob and I went into business together . . ."

"That's what I thought," said Ida. "Mr. Scrooge, I'm going to tell you a secret most Christians don't know. Most Jews are deeply opposed to religious conversion, I'm talking *either* way now. They don't want to be pestered by evangelists and they aren't looking for converts, either, not that Christians are lining up to become Jews, who needs trouble if you're not born to it?

"So what I'm saying is, if your Mr. Marley converted for business reasons, don't you think deep down it might have bothered him? I could be wrong, it's possible it didn't. But this thing you're asking Paulie to do, no, no, you could not begin to imagine how he would feel disguising his identity every day with such a lie. Each morning getting up he'd have to look in the mirror at the face of a hypocrite, every evening going to bed, he'd be laying down with a heavy heart."

A long silence. Scrooge passed a weary hand across his forehead. He tried to think of some argument to raise, but nothing came to mind. He knew in his heart that she was right.

Dr. Hopkins stepped forward to urge his patient to return to bed, but suddenly, there came a pounding at the outer door.

Fred hurried to open it. Seconds later, Timothy Cratchit dashed into the room, out of breath.

"Paulie —" he gasped. "He's in trouble!"

Ida jumped up. *"Is he hurt?"*

or days, Scrooge's young friends had been going the rounds of every London playhouse, large, small, public or private, in an attempt to find Bartie MacGregor, in hopes of learning from him the whereabouts of his erstwhile lover, Amanda Wilkins.

The sole remaining theatre on their itinerary was situated in a neighbourhood of such doubtful character that they'd put it off till last, but their fruitless endeavours finally forced them to turn their attention and footsteps to the bottom of the list.

Now one must search assiduously for Little Scarton Lane on the Surrey side of Waterloo Bridge. It consists of two shabby rooming houses, a shabby pub called The Bramble Bush and next door to it, a shabby theatre owned by the equally shabby actor-manager Sir Horatio Alfred St. Julien, alias Alf Loggins in the days when he served as dresser to Mr. Dion Boucicault.

Neither Timothy nor Paulie had a map to guide

them. They wandered for an hour, retracing their route until at length Paulie declared that they must attempt a particularly disreputable alley without a sign at its corner that they'd earlier avoided because Timothy said it looked too run-down to be the site of a theatre. He was indeed correct, but, reluctantly following his friend some little distance down its meandering reaches, Timothy soon perceived, branching off from this anonymous artery, an even more disreputable street that turned out to be Little Scarton Lane.

Timothy's nose wrinkled at the sulphur-stink of cabbage, stale beer and fresh stale that pervaded the street. With his stout ash walking-stick, he carefully stepped around, over or away from piles of trash and offal, which taxed his lame leg.

Passing The Bramble Bush, Tim stopped at a dilapidated edifice plastered with hand-drawn posters, ornate but poorly spelled, that announced the ambitious programme to be performed there that evening: *The Tragicall Hystery of Julius Ceasar, The Unknown Cavern, Romeo and Juliet Triumphant,* and *Fortune for the Asking, or The Vilanny of the Jew Barnabas.* He ran his eyes and forefinger down the list of actors comprising the collective Dramatis Personae. "Here he is, Paulie . . . look, Bart MacGregor.'

His companion joined him in perusing the poster. "'So, uncle, there you are.'"

Timothy tried the door. It would not open. He knocked, got no answer. "Somebody ought to be in there, rehearsing for tonight." He shouted hello, but to no avail, so he rapped again smartly, and this time, rusty hinges creaking, the door swung inward. Tim went through, followed by Paulie. They stepped into a mouldy vestibule covered by a dingy rectangle that once had been a purple carpet. They entered the main theatre, though it was hyperbolic to call so minor a chamber a main anything.

The theatre was furnished with a quantity of stools and chipped wooden chairs; there were six oil lamps round a single tier of boxes, and everywhere they looked they witnessed an abundance of dirt and an absence of paint.

As they approached the front of the house, Timothy heard a faint rasping sound in the wings. He sat down on the lip of the proscenium and placed his right leg upon the playing area. "Help me up over the edge, Paulie. I hear somebody snoring back there." His friend assisted him, then sprung onto the stage, and followed him into a shadowy area off left that was rich in mildew and great clotted clogs of dust.

A yelp. Timothy sprang back. "Pardon me! I didn't see you."

A chunky red-whiskered man in tattered tunic and scuffed military boots scrambled to his feet. "Well, lad," he growled, half-annoyed, half-amused, "if I catch a wink on Mither Earth, must I be trod upon like a pavin'-stone?" The speaker executed an elaborate bow. "Surr Horatio San' Jullen, at your sarvice, Surr Horatio San' Jullen, 'tis me good name, 'tis all is left me, me estates are impoverated, but y' must call me Surr Alf, for if'n y' don't, y'd be those only who doesn't." All this delivered with great rapidity of utterance, as if he were reciting some newly-discovered play of Farquhar or Sheridan.

"Pleased to meet you, sir. I'm Timothy Cratchit, this is my friend Paulie — Paul Cohen."

The thespian's smile and cordiality both widened. "Gents, I'm right glad t' make yer ackwaints. Show-time is at seven. If ye've come t' buy seats, I'm dee-leted to obleege."

"That's not why we're here," said Timothy. "We've come —"

"O' course! Surr Alf knows why, indeed!" A canny set of creases offset the manager's beetling brows. He gathered his tunic about him like Brutus. "M' company's repootation is worked its way 'cross Thames, an' here y' be, and so I say, lads, buy seats to-night, an' t'morrow I'll read y' both. I've a mind t' do Shylock, an' Tim'thy, y' got a aspeck o' Launceelot Gobbo, an' Powell here mought do yer dad and dooble Tubal and Duke o' Venice."

"I'm a little young for those parts, don't you think?"

"Not at all, Powell, not at all, stage magic: we'll slap a wig on y' 'n' smear soap 'n' whit'ning on yer eyebrows."

"But we didn't come to be actors," Timothy objected. "We're here to speak with one of your company."

Sir Alf sighed; this well-dressed pair seemed resolute in their determination not to purchase seats. But then he brightened: "Well, lads, that's all right, at the end o' the show there'll be ample opportunity t' speak t' anysome-ever! Now it's one crown for boxes, two shillin's per capitation front rows, one shillin' per last three."

The boys exchanged a glance and a nod. Paulie paid four shillings from their petty cash fund to the showman, who paid them the compliment of biting the coins before pocketing them.

"No offense, sir," said Timothy, "but we can't wait till the end of the program. Our families expect us back before then."

"All right, who is it yer wishin' t' talk to?"

"His name is Bartholomew MacGregor. Bart MacGregor."

"Bartie, is it?" Sir Alf frowned. "What's that rascal gone and done *now*?" He banished the question with a sweep of his hand. "The less I know, the better. This way, lads, I'll take y' to Bartie's offuss. This time o' day, Bartie's usually playin' commerce."[1]

1   A game similar to poker.

ir Alf stepped into the playing area of the stage, eased himself off the end of the proscenium apron, and started up the aisle of the theatre. They hurried after him. When he reached the front door, Sir Alf went through, turned and proceeded a few steps to the right, jerking his head for them to follow him into The Bramble Bush.

Timothy waited for Paulie to take the lead, but for some reason this neighbourhood seemed to make his friend hang to the rear, so Tim entered the public house first and saw a small chamber furnished with a blazing fireplace, three unfinished wooden tables with a pair of chairs at each, and exits to the rear and to the right; Sir Alf chose the latter, opening the door and gesturing for his companions to pass through.

Tim flinched at the bar's rank odour and noise. The air, smoky-thick, was heavy with sweat, to-bacco, and liquor. In one corner a pair of unshaven men in antiquated livery sat murmuring secrets they wanted no one else to hear, and they got their wish, for they were the only patrons who kept their voices down. A hard-faced girl wearing an apron that only a supreme act of faith could ever imagine once to have been white tramped back and forth from the rough tables and their rougher patrons to the bar and back again with pints of ale and an occasional shot-glass of gin.

Through an alcove, Timothy noticed two young men playing darts, and three more seated at a baize-covered table gambling at cards.

"Better wait out the 'and, Bartie ain't pleasant in'errupted," said Sir Alf. "Truth, he ain't pleasant in any sitawation, period. You lads wait up, I'll draw 'im out at the bes' propitiatin' moment."

With that, Sir Alf went into the gaming alcove and waited for the hand to be played out, and for all the bets to be settled, before presuming to approach a stocky young man with an unruly mat of pale yellow hair and sharp black eyes.

As this personage, who looked to be in his early twenties, heard the manager's message, he swivelled round and shot a glance at the boys that seemed to Tim as piercing as the twin points of a pitchfork. Bartie rose from his chair and swaggered towards them.

Perhaps Tim saw a slight movement from the corner of his eye as Paulie stiffened, or perhaps he heard the swift audible intake of his friend's breath, but suddenly Timothy sensed that something unpleasant was about to happen.

"What do y' want?" Bartie demanded, glaring at Tim. "I don't know you, an' I don't know yer crook-nose friend."

"Oh, we've met before." Paulie spoke very quietly.

"I ain't talkin' t' you, Jew-boy!"

SMACK!

It happened so fast, Timothy couldn't do a thing to stop it. One fist drove into Bartie's stomach, one smashed into his jaw, both fists double-clubbed the base of his neck. With a grunt and a groan, he crumpled into a heap on the greasy floor, and lay still.

Every head turned to see what had happened, but no one made any effort to help the victim, not even those he'd been playing cards with. Only the bar-maid moved closer. She looked down at Bartie and up at his assailant and declared, "I hopes y' kilt 'im!"

"Gor'blimey, lad!" Sir Alf knelt beside the fallen actor. "Y' may've done jus' that! An' me what's got a show openin' at siven!"

"My Paulie, *fighting*? NEVER!"

The cab jiggled Ida's words into a jouncing staccato. She sat next to Timothy and Bob Cratchit and across from Scrooge, who rested his pointy chin on his fists and shivered now and again.

"How much farther is it?" Ida asked.

"Four blocks south of the bridge, we're almost there," Timothy said, "but we'll have to get out at the corner, the street's too narrow to ride into." He looked at Paulie's mother. "He told me he was getting even."

"*Even?*" she shrilled. "Even with *what?*"

"Patience," Scrooge tried to comfort her. "I have faith that whatever Paulie did was justified."

"To strike out with his fists? There is *no* justification for that! That's what his father, God rest his soul, would say!"

Timothy tried to defend his friend by pointing out that he had been provoked by Bartie's inflammatory remarks, but Ida just shook her head more vigorously. "Since when does a Jew hit out because he's called a Jew? Naah, it's wrong, it's wrong, it's *wrong!*"

The cab slowed and stopped. Timothy led them down Little Scarton Lane and stopped in front of The Bramble Bush. "This is where it happened."

Scrooge put Ida's hand in Timothy's. "Wait out here. Bob and I will do what we can to sort things out." With his partner at his elbow, Scrooge entered the tavern, where he and Bob Cratchit saw a husky man with a black eye and puffy lips standing in an alcove. A number of other men cordoned off his passage to the main room, where Paulie sat at the far end, nursing bruised knuckles; he was in the company of a red-haired gentleman who, to Scrooge's amazement, was dressed in a dirty Roman toga and army boots.

When Paulie saw his benefactor, he hung his head in shame.

"Your mother," said Scrooge, "is outside. She's upset."

"I don't blame her."

"Timothy claims you were provoked by the things he said."

"If it was only that, I would have tolerated it."

"This Bartie — was he the thug who robbed and beat you that Christmas when you begged money for medicine for your mother?"

Paulie nodded. "The hateful things he said today brought it vividly back to me. Something snapped; before I knew it, he was on the floor. But it didn't help. There was no victory. I felt dirty."

Scrooge's arm circled Paulie's shoulder. "Some injuries never can be righted." He turned to Bob Cratchit. "Buy off that scoundrel, whatever it costs."

Paulie protested. "Mr. Scrooge, this is my responsibility!"

"It is, and you will repay me, but not in cash."

"How, then?"

"We'll talk about it later. Now, Bob, do as I say, and offer him a premium in addition to damages, if he can tell us the whereabouts of Dick Wilkins's granddaughter."

Armed with a thick black leather wallet, Bob Cratchit crossed the tap-room and opened negotiations with Mr. Bartholomew MacGregor.

Sir Alf, who had been listening to Scrooge with undivided attention, suddenly wailed, "But what about me performance? Bartie's too puff-faced to put on makeup. Powell, y' mus' go on to-night, script in 'and!"

Paulie objected. "I'm not an actor!"

"We won't stick at that, we needs a body what can speak!"

Scrooge asked how many seats Sir Alf expected to sell, and at what price. "When my partner is finished with MacGregor, I shall instruct him to buy out to-night's performance, which you may muddle through or cancel, as you wish, but this young man's mother is waiting for him outside."

The actor-manager bowed handsomely. "They says that the show mus' go on, but this be a set o' mitigratin' circumferences. Never let it be said that Surr Horatio Alf San' Jullen stood in the way o' maternal love!"

Two days before Christmas, Ebenezer Scrooge stayed late in bed; his sleep had been dreamless save for one brief flash of Father Macclesfield, suffused with baleful light, somberly regarding him where he lay.

Staring out at the bright December sky, he told himself, *this is the day my most necessary project comes to a head. I pray it does not miscarry.*

Congestion gripped his chest. Wheezing, Scrooge jingled a small bell his nephew had thoughtfully placed by his bed-side when it became apparent that his enfeebled state might warrant assistance during the night.

The tinkling summoned Fred's wife. She inquired how Scrooge had spent the evening, then, after a few hurried tidyings and neatenings, left the chamber to return with a tray laden with kippers, eggs, tomatoes, toast, milk and tea, which she set at a table by the window. "You must be excited about to-day," she observed as Scrooge sat down to break his fast.

"Indeed, I am. But I'm worried, too. Poor Dick —
I hope he's the kind of man I think he is."

A fit of coughing seized him; when it ran its
course, he had scant energy to pick at his food.
Scrooge stared listlessly at the snowy sky.

*Dr. H. might well be right; I may not hold out till
Christmas.*

Bob Cratchit met the morning coach. As he
guided Dick Wilkins to a waiting vehicle, he reassured him that Mr. Scrooge had really found his
granddaughter, and she was in good health.

The site of the momentous meeting was neither
Scrooge's home nor office, nor was it the grimy
chamber behind a blacking factory that they had
found Amanda living in. The cab bore the men north
along the perimeter of Hyde Park until, at its upper
margin, it veered northeast and rolled a short distance in that direction before stopping in front of an
attractive edifice with white steps ascending to a
door crowned with a semicircular fanlight.

Ebenezer Scrooge, muffled up in greatcoat, hat
and scarf, waited for them on the sidewalk. "Dick,
dear Dick!" he exulted, "I had not hoped to set eyes
upon you again in this world!"

"She's really well?" He wrung both of Scrooge's
hands.

"Rather anxious, but eagerly awaiting you
within —"

"What is this handsome place?" Dick Wilkins

asked.

"A modest property I own. Now, before this reunion occurs, I beseech you to compose yourself."

"I am ready for whatever transpires."

"Her circumstances," Bob Cratchit said, mounting the front steps and producing a key, "are much improved since we found her."

"Still, my dear fellow," said Scrooge, retaining his grasp of Dick's hands, "you must prepare yourself . . ."

They passed through the portal into a cheery alcove with a door that was shut on the left, while ahead a flight of seventeen steps ascended to the first floor. As Dick Wilkins waited for Scrooge to catch up with him, he heard from behind the closed portal a new noise as old as the human race itself.

"Wait!" He stopped Bob Cratchit before he could rap at the door. He turned to Scrooge. "It is as I feared."

"Feared, Dick? *Feared?*"

Dick Wilkins nodded. "The cause of her initial departure, the absence of communication, the dearth of details in the letter you wrote to fetch me — I could not close my eyes to the possibility."

Scrooge began what was intended to be a sigh, but it altered course and became a fit of coughing.

"Ebenezer," Dick said, patting his back, "you're not well!"

"Never mind me. What of Amanda? Can you forgive her?"

Now it was Dick Wilkins's turn to breathe deeply. "Oh, my dear friend, would I have journeyed this long way to chastise my own flesh and blood? Remember Fezziwig, whose offspring I wed, and recollect the joy with which he greeted this holy season! Hearken! Ebenezer, 'tis nearly Christmas! Hear the cries of another innocent!"

With eyes both moist and merry, Scrooge smiled and said, "Come in, then, Dick, come in, and meet your great-granddaughter!"

Tears, hugs, laughter. After the presentation of the new-born, Dick tugged both his ear and the margin of his waistcoat, but could not summon up the courage to speak, so Scrooge took him aside and did it for him.

"You're thinking of the difficulties that Amanda and Martha would face if they returned home with you, are you not?"

"Yes, Ebenezer. Tongues wag, and wickedly." Another tug at ear and waistcoat. "I shudder to think what this sweet babe must endure when she grows old enough to understand. I live in a small community. There I could meet their material needs comfortably, but I'd be severely taxed if I had to maintain a second household for them in another place."

"Be of good cheer, Dick. I've provided for them."

His friend shook his head. "We cannot accept charity."

"I would not insult you by offering it. This apartment building, I said, belongs to me. I've engaged Amanda to manage it as its landlady." Scrooge kept to himself the fact that he'd also instructed Bob Cratchit to draw up a deed of gift for little Martha, upon her attaining legal maturity, to this same property on the two hundred block of Baker Street.

"Oh, dear Ebenezer," Dick Wilkins said, "you are too good! How ever may I thank you?"

"Hush, gentle Dick, hush. I'm the one who benefits most. I feel as if a heavy burden has been newly lifted from my spirit."

Another coughing fit seized him.

"Ebenezer," Dick put a hand to his forehead. "you're burning up with fever!"

Scrooge gestured to Bob Cratchit. "Bob, please take me home. To-night, dear friends, I shall sleep soundly."

The friends hugged once more, then Scrooge's junior partner escorted the old man home so he might rest up before Christmas.

Flushed with pleasure, though weak with the efforts of the long day, Scrooge took to bed as soon as he got back. He donned a warm night-gown and cap, breathed medicated vapours from a porcelain bowl draped with a thick towel, a process arranged to Dr. Hopkins's specifications, then slipped between the sheets.

In one more night, he reflected, it would be

Christmas Eve. The house would be boisterous with arrivals, gifts, and carols over mugs of hot punch, but now, this night, with Dick reunited with his grandchild and reconciled to her living in London with infant Martha, now, this night before the blessed eve of the Nativity, Scrooge could muster up good spirits a-plenty. He regretted that Ida had frustrated his proposition to adopt Paulie, but already Scrooge had Bob Cratchit working on an alternative plan.

One night of rest, Scrooge thought, *One blessed night of untroubled slumber, have I not earned it? And tomorrow will be grand, and Christmas will be grander!*

He closed his eyes and swiftly fell asleep.

Rough voices and the stamping of booted feet. A glare of torchlight lit the room. Scrooge raised his head and saw that the far end of the chamber had turned into a moonless country road.

A knot of seven burly men in coarse trousers, black shirts, and thick military boots hauled a struggling, kicking bundle that their torches revealed to be a thin old man whom the roughnecks dragged through the dust by his white beard.

Scrooge could not see the victim's face, but remembering his own tombstone shown to him by the Ghost of Christmas Yet to Come, thought perhaps that this old man, too, was himself, condemned to suffer such brutality unless . . .

Unless — what?

The ruffians dropped their burden, stooped over with their torches, and set him on fire. The old man screamed, and so did Scrooge. As their victim moaned and twisted and writhed in agony, the villains shook their heads and sneered and then shouted, "He trusted in God that He would deliver Him; let Him deliver him, if He delight in him!"

As they laughed and jeered, the old men, the one in bed and the one in the nightmare, screamed and screamed and screamed.

"*Uncle, uncle! Wake up!*" Fred crashed through the door and rushed inside. His wife was right behind him.

Scrooge's eyes were wild. His forehead glistened with sweat. He muttered something over and over.

"Fred, what's he trying to tell us?"

Her husband brought his ear close to his uncle's lips. "He's saying, 'the Great Wrong.'"

She drew closer, and heard the rest of it.

"*I know! I know!*" said Scrooge, over and over and over again, "the Great Wrong . . . at last, *at last, I KNOW!*"

Stave Four

THE LAST OF THE SPIRITS

Little Fan woke the morning before Christmas and knew there was something wrong. The house was too quiet. All the usual noises were in evidence, but oddly hushed: the scurrying of feet that did their best not to tread too hard; the opening and closing of the front door, a soft sibilant shushing rather than the brisk slamming her young ears had early learned to associate with the busy bustling preparations of the year's most wonderful holiday.

"Mama," she asked as her mother entered her bedroom to help her get dressed, "is Uncle Scrooge going to die to-day?"

Her mother bustled about, opening and closing drawers to afford herself time to weigh her answer before replying. "Sooner or later, darling," she told the child, "we all must die."

"Why, Mama?"

"Because otherwise we'd never get to Heaven."

Her daughter caught her hand. "Mama, let's not go! Let's just stay here, for ever and ever!"

"Child, you're talking nonsense, and on the day before Christmas, too! Why, even our blessed Lord Jesus had to die."

Little Fan's small brows contracted. "Mama, couldn't he have asked His Father to let him live?"

Her mother looked out at the new snow. How could she answer a question that from an older mouth might be considered blasphemous?

She set out an array of holiday clothing on the bed. "Get dressed, Fan."

aulie received a message asking him to come to Mr. Scrooge's home immediately. His mother, still uncomfortable about the old man's attempt to adopt her son, warily said, "He wouldn't be inviting you to celebrate with him? It's almost Christmas."

"Mama, he wouldn't do that. But it must be important."

"I hope he's all right," she said, helping her son with his coat and cap.

crooge, after sufficiently regaining his composure, slept fitfully through the morning, but though awake by noon, he felt very weak, and kept to his bed. Downstairs, festive preparations continued; delivery boys came and went with foodstuffs, close and distant relatives and friends arrived with merry greetings on their lips. Fred, though he was fretfully concerned for the health and comfort of his uncle, did nothing to curb the good spirits of his guests; Scrooge had instructed him otherwise, and Dr. Hopkins agreed because he felt that the sounds of Christmas might buoy up his patient's spirit.

Paulie's arrival coincided with Bob Cratchit's. Fred went upstairs and tapped gently at the door. Dr. Hopkins opened it, finger to his lips. "He's asleep now."

Fred tried to steer them back downstairs, but Bob insisted that they go in. "Mr. Scrooge said to bring Paulie at once."

Dr. Hopkins did not budge. "He needs to rest."

"Soon I shall." The weak voice emerged from a thick pile of blankets. "Paulie, help me sit up. Bob, where's Tim?"

"Downstairs," Bob answered.

"Call him up, please. I want him beside me, too."

In a matter of seconds, Paulie and Tim were in the room standing on either side of Scrooge's bed, each holding one of his hands.

"Bob," the old man murmured, "please proceed."

"Master Paul," Bob began, "are you aware that Mr. Scrooge offered to adopt you to secure you a good education?"

"My mother told me," said Paulie. "I am pleased by Mr. Scrooge's generous offer, but it would be wrong of me to accept."

"Yes," Scrooge feebly agreed.

"Master Paul," Bob Cratchit continued, "you are aware of Mr. Scrooge's concern that he has left something significant undone?"

"That's why Tim and I went north with him."

"And that's why we tracked down Dick Wilkins's daughter," Timothy added. "I should have thought the satisfactory conclusion of that business would afford Mr. Scrooge the peace of mind he assuredly deserves."

"It assuredly did not," said Scrooge. "Bob, continue."

His junior partner nodded. "Mr. Scrooge is determined that you, Master Paul, shall have an education at least equivalent to that of a Christian youth of your age, class and character —"

"Better, Bob! Better!" Scrooge exclaimed before succumbing to a violent bout of coughing.

A pause till Scrooge recovered; a rattle, then, of documents unfolded. "Toward this end, Master Paul," said Cratchit, "this is the new plan Mr. Scrooge has set in motion."

The youth swiftly scanned the sheaf of legal foolscap.

"What does it say?" Tim asked.

Paulie handed back the papers. "Mr. Scrooge has offered a princely sum to Charlotte Montefiore to begin a Jewish college of higher learning, provided only that I be its first pupil."

"Is this proposition acceptable?" Bob inquired.

Paulie looked at Scrooge's nephew and saw puzzled doubt in Fred's eyes. Paulie wanted to say yes, but like the Scottish laird's Amen, the word stuck in his throat.

Bob Cratchit saw his hesitation. "Consider carefully. You would only be the first of many beneficiaries."

Across the bed, Tim projected with silent urgency the plea that his friend speak the affirmative word the old man wanted so much to hear from his lips . . .

"If this will help other J —" Paulie paused, editing himself. "If this will help other *Englishmen,* I shall gratefully accept Mr. Scrooge's offer."

Scrooge smiled. His voice was little more than an aspirate whisper. "Thank you, that's one more burden lifted from my spirit. Now, Bob, Fred, and you, Doctor Hopkins . . . leave me alone with these young gentlemen."

Dr. Hopkins felt his patient's pulse and listened to his heart. "It would be best if you rested."

Scrooge beckoned him closer; the physician bent over so that his ear was close to his patient's mouth. "If I rest now," the old man asked, "can you guarantee that I will have time later?" The doctor shook his head. "I thought not. Therefore, please honour my wishes."

At a gesture and a nod from Dr. Hopkins, Bob quitted the room and went downstairs, but Fred only withdrew as far as the threshold, where he stayed with the physician, in case Scrooge should suddenly need them.

"Boys," said Scrooge, "there are two packages in my bureau. They're meant for you."

Tim fetched small boxes tied with identical gold ribbons and covered in glittery foil, and passed one to Paulie. The wrappings were off in a jiffy, and the contents revealed: two handsome pocket watches with jewelled actions, each alike in cost and design.

"Merry Christmas, Tim. Happy Hanukkah, Paulie. Did I get the date right?"

"Yes, Mr. Scrooge. This year, the holidays overlap. They don't always. Hanukkah is a moveable feast."

"I know. Jacob Marley told me that a long time ago." A curious restlessness quivered within his voice; he looked at Timothy, then Paulie. "It's him, you know."

"Him?" they echoed.

"*The Great Wrong!*" Scrooge collapsed upon his pillow. "The one Great Wrong unrighted. Jacob, my partner, my friend, my — *saviour.*"

A long silence. The boys stood by his side, mutely holding onto his hands. Scrooge's eyes closed.

After a time, Timothy said, "He feels so cold."

"Doctor," said Paulie, "I think you'd better come here."

Dr. Hopkins felt for a pulse. He laid the cold hand on the coverlet. He stopped Paulie from taking it again, and suggested to Tim that he also release his hold.

"But he has to know we're here!" he objected.

Paulie, noting the physician's concern, gently tugged his friend's hand. "Tim, it may do more good if we just rest our hands lightly over his, like this." He placed his palm over the back of the old man's fingers. Tim paused, then followed his example.

Dr. Hopkins sighed, relieved that there was no danger to the boys from the death-clutch of *rigour mortis.*

Fog, not at all like London. Wisps of half-remembered promises, half-forgotten hopes, a curlicue of better times, memories of Christmas trees and the intermingled gift of laughter and tears.

When the clouds lifted, Scrooge beheld a prospect so dazzling his eyes had to close again till his world-darkened senses adjusted to that Primal Light that contains within itself all brilliancies, colours, glows, shades and tints, intentions and connotations.

Were there heavenly gates?

There were. No filigree compromised their design, nor were they worked in iron or brass or any other earthly metal; they were a function of the Light.

Were they studded with pearls?

Yes, but not the dusky silver found in earth's seas: rosy orbs, rather, blended with omnipresent glory.

But the Heavenly Gates were shut tight.

Scrooge, to tell the truth, was a bit disappointed. *How can this be?* he wondered. The difference between the plane he was on and the place he'd left behind was profound. There, truth was shrouded in mystery; here, all things unanswered would surely be satisfied. There, the very business of living exhausted the mortal flesh that contained it; here, the rifts and tides of energy that tore and buffeted our little world flowed abundantly and at peace, and the crooked was made straight, and the rough places plain.

And yet, Ebenezer Scrooge was still disappointed.

The Light became a mighty whirlwind. From its midst there came a Voice he felt as much as heard.

SPEAK YOUR THOUGHT.

"Is this *all?*" Scrooge asked. "Christopher Wren has done nearly as well, you know."

YOU RECKON BY THE WORLD'S RELIANCE ON FORM. HERE, ONLY WHAT YOU SEE IS FALSE.

Paradox is not an answer, Scrooge thought, *but let it go. Where's my sister? And shall I meet once more my beloved Belle?*

THEY ARE WITHIN. YOUR CASE HAS NOT YET BEEN JUDGED.

From this, Scrooge perceived that both words and thoughts were heard in this place. And now, the Gates vanished, the mighty Light dimmed, and he found himself in the dusty fore-chamber of an ordinary-looking business office. A dry little clerk rummaged through a shelf crammed with huge tattered ledgers. He drew one down, and Scrooge saw in raised letters on the volume's spine:

EBENEZER SCROOGE.

"Be seated. They'll be ready for you presently."

Scrooge did as he was told. In his early days on earth, he mused, he often had to wait on the leisure of those placed above him, for that's the world's way, compounded in England by a system designed to perpetuate the predominancy of the upper classes.

After what seemed to him like an interminable wait, he addressed the clerk. "I should have thought that things would happen swiftly here."

"You'd think so, wouldn't you?" that worthy replied with a dry chuckle, rubbing his palms together as if kindling a small fire. "But here, time is a relative proposition. Your present impatience reflects earthly conditioning. You'll adjust."

"Perhaps," Scrooge said, but thought, *Bureaucracies, when they grow inefficient, excuse themselves in this fashion.*

"True enough," the clerk agreed. "Nevertheless, in these parts, time is a concurrency."

"Can you hear *everything* I think?"

"Thoughts, words, deeds — all proclaim themselves aloud."

With that, the venue abruptly changed. Suddenly Scrooge found himself on a bench near the dock of a great chamber like Courtroom Number One, Old Bailey. A quorum of jurors filed in, and a magistrate in black robes and white wig assumed his place.

"EBENEZER SCROOGE." His name reverberated across the vaulting arch of the firmament. He rose and entered the dock.

A handsome woman who resembled a portrait Scrooge's father had shown him of the mother he never knew, addressed the bench.

"The defendant's life," she said, "was not blameless, but early suffering laid the groundwork for his ultimate salvation."

With that, the events and deeds of Scrooge's life flickered in the air like a magic lantern show. Scrooge, with the perspective of an auditor at a West End pageant, perceived how parental abandonment, soon followed by his sister's death, led him to draw away from Belle and put away all feelings except the love of cold, undying cash. And Scrooge remembered with renewed force how Jacob Marley hid his better nature the same way, Jacob, the friend whose passing he had refused to mourn.

The years flickered by: Scrooge's ghostly conversion and that glorious Christmas morning when he met Paulie and took the first steps to save Tiny Tim's life, and many acts of charity since then, on up to those efforts that culminated in reuniting Dick Wilkins with his grandchild Amanda and her infant daughter Martha.

The Defense Attorney sat down, and a man who greatly resembled Father Macclesfield stood before the bench.

The Prosecutor said, "We stipulate that the defendant, once warned of his impending fate, made the best use he could of his remaining time on earth. This court now must determine whether these latter-day efforts, if we may so call them, were enough to excuse his multitude of earlier sins."

"The jury will consider its verdict," the magistrate said.

Scrooge expected another lengthy delay, but hardly were the words out of the magistrate's mouth than the foreman of the jury stood and declared, "We have."

The magistrate regarded Scrooge benignly. "Is the defendant prepared to hear the judgment of this tribunal?"

"I am."

"Then what is the jury's decision?"

"Ebenezer Scrooge," said the foreman of the jury, "Thou art weighed in the balance, and *not* found wanting."

The courtroom vanished and, as the foreman's words rang through illimitable space, Scrooge found himself before the Heavenly Gates, and they were open, and on the other side, a radiant smile on her sweet face, stood his sister with outstretched arms . . .

But Ebenezer Scrooge said, "No. I *cannot* enter."

red stood in the bedroom, his hand held by his wife. That eloquence his uncle once ironically suggested might lead him to Parliament was not in evidence; Fred had no words now, only tears.

Dr. Hopkins attempted to comfort him. "Your uncle lived a goodly span."

Fred grieved.

"The change of heart you told me of made his latter years blessed."

Fred nodded, but still grieved.

"I did my best to prepare you," the physician apologized, puzzled by the strength of Fred's emotion. "His failing health —"

"Doctor," Fred's wife said gently, "you must understand — Mr. Scrooge was the only living person who still remembered my husband's mother."

And there was Fan, a radiant smile upon her sweet face, her arms open. Scrooge yearned to run to them, to *come home*. Instead he said, "No. I *cannot* enter."

Time froze. Hatch-marks worried the margins of Light. A frown clouded his sister's brow; her lips shaped a question even as the Whirlwind arose and the Voice within spoke.

THE GATES ARE WIDE; YOUR GOOD DEEDS HAVE EARNED YOUR SALVATION.

"I cannot enter," said Scrooge, "until I rectify that last Great Wrong that troubled me during my final days on earth."

THAT TIME IS PAST. OTHERS SHALL FOLLOW WHERE YOU LED.

Scrooge stood firm. "No one else will elect to speak on behalf of Jacob Marley!"

JACOB MARLEY HAS BEEN WEIGHED IN THE BALANCE AND FOUND WANTING.

"It isn't fair," Scrooge argued.

A flicker in the Light, a low moaning, but when

the Voice in the Whirlwind sounded, it was resolute.

JUDGMENT HAS ALREADY BEEN ENTERED AGAINST HIM. MARLEY'S PENANCE IS ETERNAL.

"*No! He must be tried again!*"

Dark clouds billowed menacingly.

WHO IS THIS THAT DARKENETH COUNSEL BY WORDS WITHOUT KNOWLEDGE?

Scrooge began to tremble at this, but still he would not be swayed. "A priest instructed me in my duty. I *must* rescue Jacob!"

YOU, WHO BARELY ESCAPED JACOB MARLEY'S FATE?

"I regret my sins," he replied humbly, "but still plead to be heard. I feel I can offer important new evidence on Jacob's behalf. Have I not heard preachers proclaim that mercy is the most blessed attribute of divinity?"

The tempest died. The skies brightened. The Voice spoke.

IT SHALL BE SO.

The Gates closed, shutting Fan from view. Scrooge found himself back in court. The jury box was still full, but the prisoner's dock was empty.

An old man in robes and wig, carrying a large legal tome stepped behind the bench and sat upon a cosmic wool-sack. Scrooge thought he looked remarkably like Old Fezziwig.

"Summon the Defendant," the Lord High Chancellor told the Bailiff, who called out his name.

"JACOB MARLEY!"

And Marley materialized in the dock. The last time Scrooge set mortal eyes on him, his friend was an insubstantial ghost, but now he looked as solid as if he were still alive: the same pigtail, waistcoat, tights, boots, their tassels bristling in the cold wind that tormented him even here, tossing his coatskirts and the braid of his hair. Chains of metal wound about his middle and over his shoulders and shackled his legs, and locked to the links were cashboxes, keys, padlocks, ledgers, deeds, and purses wrapped in steel. Marley groaned at their wearisome weight.

Scrooge approached the bench. "Your Honour, may I speak with the prisoner?"

The Lord High Chancellor smiled. "My dear Mr. Scrooge, I have followed your progress on earth with keen interest, especially in the closing years of your life. The good deeds you've accomplished live after you. They have earned for your friend Mr. Marley this unprecedented reopening of his case. The Court grants your request to speak with the Defendant before the trial. However, you must not touch him, or in any way attempt to ease his burden."

Scrooge crossed to the dock. In spite of the judge's warning, he almost forgot himself and hugged his old partner and companion, but Marley, perceiving his intention, shrank from his touch.

"Ebenezer, would you share my wretched lot? You must do nothing to assist me in my just punishment!"

"My dear friend, you have a chance at last to escape!"

Marley dolefully moaned, "No hope remains for me, Ebenezer."

"We'll see about that. But we've been granted a brief time to converse. There are two things I need to talk to you about."

"Speak. Demand. I'll answer."

"My first item of business requires no reply. I simply wish to thank you for that work of reclamation you undertook on my behalf. I admit that at first I was not enthusiastic over the prospect of being haunted three times, but when I fell down upon the gravestone that bore my name and it turned into my own bedpost — when I knew I still could wipe out the shadow of that future Christmas, I regretted you were not there to witness my rebirth."

"But I was! They permitted me to see that wonderful morning. It was the sole joy I've experienced since my lonely death."

"Oh, Jacob, Jacob, how cruelly you've suffered."

"My punishment is what I myself earned."

"But not for all Eternity!"

"Whoever shall look upon a Great Wrong and take no action, shall bear his portion of that Great Wrong for *all time!*"

Scrooge shivered at the reminder.

Marley's chains rattled. "You had two things to discuss?"

"Yes. The second is a matter of personal curiosity. When you converted to Christianity, did you do so out of spiritual conviction?"

Marley frowned. "You already know the answer to that, Ebenezer. Though I will admit some small part of me found solace in the tale of the Wise Men and the Star."

"Was it difficult to turn your back on your people, Jacob?"

"I had no people. I was a stranger. Never mind that I was born in London, I was regarded as a foreigner. Many still treated me that way, even after I converted."

"I never did!"

"No, Ebenezer, you did not. Like me, you cared for nothing but money."

The Lord High Chancellor tapped his gavel. "Mr. Scrooge, it is time to begin. I must ask you to step away from the dock."

"Courage, Jacob!" Scrooge said, and took his place behind a table reserved for barristers.

How may an earthly author presume to act as journalist to the mysteries of celestial justice? — *H. M. Rex* (so we imperfectly imagine) *vs. Jacob Marley, a continuance.* And yet the gentle Bard of Avon hints with convincing authority at the workings of Heavenly Justice in his grand ghost story of the Danish usurper Claudius who, unable to pray, admits that there is no shuffling in the Great Court above, for there the guilty must be prepared to give in evidence even to the very teeth and forehead of their faults.

Thus, Jacob Marley's retrial began with the Defendant's own testimony: "I frittered away my mortal existence accruing money to no purpose, for I spent no more than a pittance for my lodgings and sustenance. Save for my friendship with my partner, I turned my back on mankind and made no effort to employ my worldly goods in bettering the lot of those less fortunate than I. I hardened my heart to human suffering; I had neither compassion nor charity, and left no legacy of loving-kindness to ensure for myself a place amongst the blessed. For these grievous faults, I am compelled to walk through Eternity, borne down by these impediments."

Here Marley shook his chains and moaned. "But the worst of my punishment is that everywhere I go, I witness mortal misery that I am powerless to banish from the earth. Because I hastened through life without mercy, all time is mine now to repent." Another groan, another clattering of chains, keys, padlocks, ledgers.

The Lord High Chancellor nodded to Ebenezer Scrooge. "Kindly state the case for the Defense."

Scrooge rose. "Your Honour, am I permitted to call witnesses?"

"If they are alive, you may only reference them. Their value, however, shall receive full weight in this court."

So Scrooge referenced Paulie and Ida Cohen, Timothy and Bob Cratchit, his nephew Fred, Dick Wilkins and his family, and the gentlemen who solicited him to contribute to the poor at Christmastime, at first to be rebuffed by the miser he once was. The list continued; Scrooge had done so much good in that decade plus a year since the Christmas Day of his spiritual salvation, he feared he would not be able to remember all those that he helped, but to his surprise and relief, every moment of his past was available to his memory to be tapped and recounted.

When the long roster of good deeds was at last completed, the Lord High Chancellor said, "You have argued handsomely for your own place in this place of joy and peace, but since that has already been secured, the enumeration just entered into evidence seems to be of no weight so far as Jacob Marley is concerned."

"I ask the court's indulgence," said Scrooge. "I shall speak to that purpose presently. But first, I wish to call my one available witness."

"Pray do so."

"I call Jacob Marley."

The prisoner, already in the dock, inclined his head.

Scrooge paused for the Bailiff to swear in the witness, but the Lord High Chancellor, reading his thought, explained there was no need. "Oaths are not necessary here. No lie may be told, for in this court all truth is revealèd. Counsel may question the witness."

Scrooge turned to Marley. "Do you remember that Christmas Eve when you visited me as a spirit?"

"I do."

"Tell the court about it, Jacob."

The Lord High Chancellor observed, "The court recorded the business in question on the occasion of its occurrence."

Scrooge argued, "My case depends upon an exact rendering of the statement that the witness made on that occasion."

"Very well," the judge said. "Proceed."

Scrooge nodded to Marley. "It was no easy thing to bring about, Ebenezer. Your heart was hard as flint. At first, you even refused to acknowledge my very existence. 'There's more of gravy than the grave about you,' those, I think, were your words."

"Then why did you bother with me at all, Jacob?"

"I saw how long the chain was that you were forging."

"And what of it? Didn't you harbour resentment at your own fate? Wasn't it satisfying to reflect that the partner of your misdeeds would eventually receive his comeuppance?"

"No, no, Ebenezer! You were my friend. I wanted to rescue you from the awful consequences that befell me."

Counsel for the Defense addressed the bench. "Let it be entered into evidence that in wishing this, Jacob Marley, though already condemned, was engaged upon a deed of unselfish charity."

"It was so noted many years ago," the judge pointed out. "It earned him the boon of being permitted to undertake your salvation."

Scrooge returned to Marley. "You sat upon an armchair and gave me timely warning. Can you recall, word for word, what you said to me that Christmas Eve?"

"I can. I said them to myself many times in preparation for that meeting."

"Please tell the court the precise words you used, Jacob."

"I said, 'I am here to-night to warn you, that you have yet a chance and hope of escaping my fate.' "

"And what else? It is crucial that you recollect everything, word for word."

"If you say so, Ebenezer." Marley did not believe Scrooge's efforts would make any difference in the cosmic balance. "I said, 'a chance and hope of escaping my fate. A chance and hope of my procuring, Ebenezer.'"

"Precisely! Let the court note his exact words: 'A chance and hope of *my* procuring.'"

"It has been noted," said the judge. "What of it?"

Scrooge said, "I ask that the court stipulate that my salvation was entirely accomplished because of Jacob Marley's labours on my behalf."

"Of what use is this to your case?"

"Is it so stipulated?" Scrooge insisted. "I can, if necessary, call the Ghosts of Christmas Past, Present, and Yet to Come as witnesses." (Scrooge was aware that this was slightly absurd, since the third spectre never seemed to utter a word.)

"There's no need. One of that trio is quite busy tonight." The judge opened his hands in a gesture of acquiescence. "For whatever it is worth, your point is so stipulated."

Scrooge returned his attention to the Defendant. "Tell me, Jacob, was this chance easy to procure?"

"No, it was not."

"How difficult was it to obtain?"

"It took me seven earthly years."

"Pursued even as you endured your own eternal sufferings? Or did those occasions when you put forth pleas on my behalf gain you any moment of relief?"

"Never an instant," said Marley. "My sins are a constant burden and cause of grief, even here in this courtroom."

"Was the idea to intercede for my soul suggested by any being, mortal or immortal, during your hellish wanderings?"

"No."

"It was wholly and solely your own thought?"

The Lord High Chancellor interrupted. "Counsel for the Defense has sufficiently emphasized the point. Is there anything else you wish to inquire of the witness?"

Scrooge shook his head.

"Then have you anything further to bring before this court?"

"Your Honour, I have. At this time, I wish to enter into evidence the roster of my own good deeds in favour of the Defendant's reclamation."

The Lord High Chancellor's fleecy eyebrows arched like a pair of cricket wickets. "Are you suggesting, sir, what I believe you to be suggesting?"

"I am suggesting that if the Defendant had not rescued me, I never would have performed any of those works of charity and good will that set my own Heavenly account in order. Not one of those deeds would have happened if it were not for his intervention. Thus every act of mercy attributed to me must also be credited upon Jacob Marley's ledgers. If Jacob Marley had not saved me, Paulie's mother would have died. If Jacob Marley had not rescued me, Tiny Tim would have died. If Jacob Marley had not —"

"Hold, enough!" the judge cried. "Mr. Scrooge, have you any further points to make?"

"Your Honour, the Defense rests."

"Your argument *has* justified the reopening of this case." He tapped his gavel. "Court is in recess whilst the jury deliberates."

And there was silence in Heaven for half an hour.

Bob Cratchit tapped at the door; Fred's wife opened it.

"Mr. Scrooge has passed on," Bob said. It was not a question.

"How did you know?" Fred asked.

"I felt him depart. I don't know how. Maybe because I spent so many years in his presence." Bob hesitated. "I should like to say goodbye."

Fred nodded. Cratchit, approaching the bed, laid a hand on his son Tim's shoulder; the youth, whose other palm still rested on Scrooge's cold hand, clasped his father's fingers in his.

Bob spoke to his departed employer. "Before you changed your heart, Mr. Scrooge, all those long hours I spent working in the bitter cold, so did you, sir, and yet at the close of each day, I at least went home to a loving wife and family. Now my good lad Timothy here will bear witness to the fact that after that splendid Christmas vision you were granted, you did wondrous things for him and the rest of my family, but —"

Cratchit's voice trembled. "But Mr. Scrooge, even when you were at your most miserly, I always sensed that deep within, you had a *good heart*."

"**E**benezer, where did you learn to think like that?"

Scrooge, who could still sense both boys' hands resting lightly on the cold fingers of his earthly relict, replied, "There is a young Jewish lad I knew who told me of his people's prophetic writings."

Enlightenment dawned on Marley's heavy features. "You argued my case with Talmudic logic!"

"If you say so. Let's just hope it worked in this Christian court." He tried to pat his friend's hand, but Marley pulled away.

"Ebenezer, *don't!*"

"What harm can it do?"

"Hush! The judge returns. The verdict's about to be declared."

The Lord High Chancellor's wig looked neatly powdered. Scrooge wondered about vanity in Heaven. *Perhaps it's only the way I see him. I'm still connected to the world of appearances. I wonder how long before a spirit relinquishes its hold upon the past?*

"It differs," said Marley, reading his thought. "That's why there are still so many ghosts on the earth."

"*Oyez . . . oyez . . . oyez . . .*"

As the Bailiff chanted, Scrooge resumed his place at the barrister's table.

The judge regarded Counsel for the Defense with speculative interest. "The prisoner's argument, which I may commend you upon, Mr. Scrooge, has been weighed and carefully, most carefully, considered. Its intrinsic worth, as well as the legal precedent it would set, have been factored into the court's decision."

Scrooge did not like the sound of that.

The Lord High Chancellor continued. "Taking your arguments into account, and giving them all the weight that they deserve, this tribunal has determined that the punishment that was meted out to Jacob Marley —"

Scrooge wondered if it was too late to pray.

"— the punishment that was meted out to Jacob Marley is deemed to be just. Because the prisoner had no knowledge or intent to bring about those good deeds that occurred as a result of his intervention in Counsel's case, these deeds must be termed benefits de mortuis, and may not be applied to prisoner's case ex post facto. Therefore court's original decision, unaltered and uncommuted, is upheld now and for all Eternity."

"*NO!*" Scrooge cried. "This is not justice! This Great Wrong cannot be perpetuated!"

"The decision of this court is final, and is not subject to further appeal." The Lord High Chancellor's voice grew stern. "Jacob Marley . . ."

The prisoner bowed his head. "Your Honour?"

"Sentence has been declared and reaffirmed. You are no longer permitted within this blessed vestibule of Paradise."

With a clank of his chains, Marley stepped out of the dock. Perceiving Scrooge's distress, he said, "Through all Eternity, I will be grateful for your efforts. When I walk the cold streets and byways of earth and witness afresh mankind's suffering, this loving deed on your part will temper my torments with some vestige of mercy. And now, dear friend and partner, forever farewell."

He shuffled slowly out of court, dragging the links and appendages of his burden.

An intrusive upsurge of the Light of Glory obliterated the courtroom. The Gates of Heaven reappeared and swung wide so that Scrooge could enter. A little way off was his beloved sister Fan, her arms wide to clasp him. Close behind her stood another woman with a smile as bright as the sun.

But Ebenezer Scrooge turned his back on the parted Gates. No voice called his name. No forestalling hand prevented him from leaving. In the distance he saw the chain-laden figure of Jacob Marley shambling down a long dusty highway that led him back to the dirty streets of London. Scrooge hurried after him, but it was a long road, and the buffeting winds of punishment sent Marley to earth before him.

Scrooge sought him in all of the paths and byways where poor men gnawed mouldy crusts of bread picked out of refuse piles, and poor women, racked with pain, coughed out their lungs in dingy cellars and unlighted doorways, and poor boys, once innocent, lurked on street-corners and picked pockets, and little girls, once innocent, plied an even harsher trade for their sustenance. Everywhere he went he saw the bitterness of poverty and the worser fate of profit without compassion, the detritus clogging the dirty streets of London, streets as foul as Barrowe Lane, where Paulie grew up, ghettos where Jews eked out a miserable existence working at tailoring or furniture-making *unless and until*, he thought, *they learn to lend money at usurious rates like Scrooge & Marley used to charge*!

He sought his friend for endless days and nights, or perhaps it was only an instant, Scrooge lost all track of time, but at length it was midnight in the City when at last he caught up with Jacob Marley.

As on that other fateful Christmas Eve, Marley was wandering hither and thither in restless haste with a company of damned souls, every one of them fettered with fathoms of iron cable, every one of them moaning in sorrow and self-accusation.

"Ebenezer!" Marley exclaimed. "What are you doing *here*?!"

"I've been searching for you ever since your trial ended."

"Why? There's nothing more that you can do for me."

"If your good deeds on my behalf bear so little weight above, I cannot accept the salvation you brought about for me."

"Ebenezer, you can't change cosmic justice."

"I must!"

"But *how*?"

How, indeed?

And *why?*

The fact of Scrooge's sacrifice bore down upon him: he had given up everything, reunion with his dear sister, that longed-for forgiveness from Belle, his very salvation . . . for what?

Or, rather, for whom?

For a converted Jew!

Scrooge's conscience smote him. In life, take him at his worst, he had never harboured such odious sentiments, but here, on the nether side of Heaven, in the wake of all he had relinquished, for one Judas moment, he dared to turn his old friend into a scapegoat, the way one did with — foreigners.

I'm worse than that oafish landlord at The Maypole!

Had he been tempted by Satan? Scrooge rejected the notion. *Don't blame Old Nick. Blame yourself. Intolerance has deep roots.*

"Ebenezer," Marley insisted, "how can you hope to alter cosmic justice?"

Good question . . . and asked by the converted Jew who engineered the very salvation you cast aside!

"I'll tell you how, Jacob . . . by emulating the example of our Lord." And as he said that, Ebenezer Scrooge knelt in the dust and grasped Marley's chains.

"NO! YOU MUSTN'T!"

"Hush, friend, hush, I shall and I must. If you

are doomed to carry this burden through all Eternity, then so am I, for in life I helped you forge this chain."

"I tried to spare you this!"

"That is precisely why I must help you, Jacob." And as he spoke, Scrooge wrapped the great shackles round his shoulders and waist. The iron links of Heaven's wrath cut harshly into him. He staggered to his feet with a groan. "Almighty God, they're heavy!" He took one tottering, painful step and then another, and now the bitter wind of damnation tore him away from Marley's side.

"*JACOB!*" he shouted, but the tempest flung him away like refuse, and when the fury died, he was nowhere near London or Jacob Marley or any other spirit.

He was utterly alone.

Scrooge understood his plight. He was free to spurn his own salvation, but was not permitted to mitigate Marley's suffering.

And yet, *No!* he realized, bleakly triumphant, *I am allowed to bear half of Jacob's chains.* His selfless act had relieved fully half of his friend's punishment; Scrooge took great comfort in that.

But where am I?

He was in a dark, dingy room in a mansion of dull red brick, with a broken weather-cock surmounting a cupola on the roof, and a bell hanging from it that would never sound again. The panels of the room were shrunken, and the windows cracked; fragments of plaster fell out of the ceiling, and the naked laths showed through, and there he was again, alone once more, when all the other boys had gone home for the jolly holidays.

I know this dreadful place! All too well . . . my old school-room as it was in life, and none left behind but me.

With a mournful shake of his chains, Scrooge walked up and down, remembering a better time when his sister Fan had come through that portal and rescued him.

If it is my fate to be confined here for all Eternity, how then may one believe in the mercy of Heaven?

The thought struck him with renewed force: he'd sacrificed everything for a friend, but now his friend was gone, and Scrooge was fettered and condemned to haunt a place of such utter misery that he equated it with Hell. All because of Jacob Marley, the ex-Jew.

"*No!* I repent that hateful thought, it is the workings of the Devil!" Scrooge cried out. "Let all Eternity pass, let my heart ache unceasingly, these chains cannot weigh as heavily as poor Jacob's merciless punishment!"

And yet Jacob Marley, at his retrial, had acknowledged and accepted the justice of his fate, maintaining to the end that it was his own deeds that had earned him the rigours of Eternity. It brought to mind the scheme of Hell forged in rhyme by the great Italian poet Dante, for Scrooge remembered his headmaster explaining that the damned souls of the Inferno had not been consigned to their fate by some cosmic tribunal, but, like water seeking its proper level, sought of their own accord whichever circles of the Pit their earthly deeds had reserved for them. A just scheme, perhaps, but devoid of mercy.

Scrooge clasped his hands and bowed his head in prayer. "Almighty God, I do not think that cosmic justice should be harsher than life itself. We poor mortals have so little time to learn to love one another. I entreat you to hear me . . . if my former blessed state permits the granting of one true prayer, then grant me mine and accept Jacob Marley into Heaven *instead* of me and permit me to carry throughout Eternity *all* of his chains . . ."

There are times in the life of the spirit when Heaven needs do nothing further. That which is blessed is instantly perceived with the heart's wisdom, and salvation flows from within. So even as Ebenezer Scrooge's true prayer flew upward, he knew with the certainty of Enlightenment that he had grasped that great lesson of Love which all mankind must teach its children if we and they are to survive the strife of nations. So peace reigned in Scrooge's bosom as the air trembled with the glory of his words.

he door of the school-room flung open and a young woman darted into the room. She threw her arms round Scrooge's neck and kissed him.

"I have come to bring you home, dear brother!" she exclaimed, brimful of glee. "To bring you home for good and all. Father is so much kinder than he used to be, and home is Heaven! I asked and was told Yes, you are never to come back here; and we'll be together ever after!"

She laughed, and began to drag him, in her eagerness, towards the door — and then they were in a place of Light, and standing beside them, still in chains, was Jacob Marley.

"Ebenezer," he whispered, "something is *happening*."

Something, indeed, was happening. The crystal dew of mercy rained down and healed their wounds. Every shackle and ledger, brazen key and hard padlock fell off. Link by link, their chains melted and for the first time since the night he died, Jacob Marley stood up straight and tall.

Weeping, shouting, hugging, laughing, Scrooge and Marley passed through the Gates, and there was Fan to greet them, and Scrooge's father and mother, and they were smiling, and Marley's parents, too, and there were the Fezziwigs, and Belle, young and beautiful, and there was rejoicing and merriment, and it was Christmas.

And Ebenezer Scrooge cried, "I haven't missed it, after all!"

"I'd better tell them downstairs," Fred said.

"No!" Paulie and Timothy exclaimed. Tim explained: "He'd want them all to enjoy the holiday. Let's let them."

"A good thought," Dr. Hopkins remarked. "A little delay will not . . . but what are you doing here, child?"

They turned and saw a pair of eyes welling up with tears.

"Uncle Scrooge is dead, isn't he?" little Fan asked.

Before her parents could speak, Doctor Hopkins knelt beside her. "We're all immortal, little girl. This is how we survive. Someday when you have a child of your own, you will understand."

"I know already," Fan said with a sniffle.

"What do you know, darling?" Her mother dried Fan's tears.

"That love never goes away."

Close to a road in a little northern town once dominated by a Benedictine monastery, there stands, high on a hill-top, a small church and a smaller cemetery. Two graves there are set close together, though not side by side, for the first was dug many years before the newer, a simple grey stone set flat in the earth, already cracked by the harsh northern winters.

Some visitors think of tombstones and tombstones and how the world runs on, uncaring, and pity the mortal buried below because he rests in an obscure plot in an obscure market town somewhere near the Welsh border. But some consider, instead, that there are people in the world at this instant whose good actions and good thoughts may be traced back to this very grave.

Each year, two young men come to visit it, and put small stones upon it for remembrance. The one who carries a cane prays aloud, and his companion meditates. But they laugh together, too, and talk fondly of the first time that each met the deceased.

"He was like a second father to me, Paulie."

"He was for me, too."

"Which means —"

"Which means —"

They take each other's hand, Christian and Jew, and complete the thought together.

"Which means we're practically brothers!"

And Timothy Cratchit said, "May that be truly said of us, and all of us, Amen."

THE END

Acknowledgments

In addition to *A Christmas Carol,* the author is indebted to certain passages of Charles Dickens's *Barnaby Rudge, Bleak House, Christmas Stories, Dombey and Son, The Old Curiosity Shop, Our Mutual Friend, The Pickwick Papers, Sketches by Boz, A Tale of Two Cities,* and "A December Vision," from the December 14, 1850, edition of *Household Words,* on which the text of Father Macclesfield's sermon is based. Father Macclesfield himself is patterned after a character from Robert Hugh Benson's scarce collection of occult tales, *A Mirror of Shallot.*

An earlier version of the opening chapter appeared i n *The Possession of Immanuel Wolf and Other Improbable Tales,* published by Doubleday in 1981.

The author acknowledges and recommends the following resources: David Feldman's *Englishmen and Jews: Social Relations and Political Culture*

1840-1914 (Yale University Press 1994), Daniel Pool's *What Jane Austen Ate and Charles Dickens Knew* (Touchstone 1993), the Forster collection at London's Victoria and Albert Museum, the Dickens House on Doughty Street, London, and the Dickens Museum in Rochester, England.

Thanks to Naomi Epel's *The Observation Deck: A Tool Kit for Writers,* and for invaluable input from John Betancourt, Carole Buggé, Saralee Kaye, H. Clark Kee, Donald Maass, and Kathy Szaj.

Author's Note: The gravestone described at the end of the story exists and may be seen in a churchyard in Shrewsbury, England. It was left there after the filming of the George C. Scott version of *A Christmas Carol.*

Marvin Kaye
New York, 2001